D0045956

MISSING OKALEE

MISSING
OKALEE

LAURA OJEDA MELCHOR

SHADOW
MOUNTAIN

Library of Congress Cataloging-in-Publication Data

Names: Melchor, Laura Ojeda, author.
Title: Missing Okalee / Laura Ojeda Melchor.
Description: Salt Lake City : Shadow Mountain, [2021] | Audience: Grades 2–3. | Summary: "When Pheobe's sister, Okalee, drowns in the river during their annual spring celebration, Phoebe is wracked with guilt to the point that she loses her singing voice"—Provided by publisher.
Identifiers: LCCN 2021013203 | ISBN 9781629729329 (hardback)
Subjects: CYAC: Sisters—Fiction. | Grief—Fiction. | Singing—Fiction | Middle schools—Fiction | Schools—Fiction. | Cuban Americans—Fiction. | Montana—Fiction. | LCGFT: Fiction.
Classification: LCC PZ7.1.M46918 Mi 2021 | DDC [Fic]—dc23
LC record available at https://lccn.loc.gov/2021013203

Printed in the United States of America
Lake Book Manufacturing, Inc., Melrose Park, IL

10 9 8 7 6 5 4 3 2 1

To my sister, Sarah, and to sisters everywhere.

1

It feels like the school gym is about to swallow me whole. My heart is a bird trapped in my rib cage. My legs are about as stable as a riverbank in the spring, muddy and on the brink of collapse. I'm staring at Ms. Loring seated at the baby grand piano on stage left so I don't have to see the students fidgeting in metal folding chairs in front of me.

Ms. Loring flips the page of her music book. She glances at me. "Ready for the note?"

I nod. She plays my opening note, a low F.

I take a deep breath and remind myself that I can do this. I can sing this solo so well that every fidgeting student will go quiet with awe. I have to if I want to be the one to sing it at the school's performance at the Grayling Crossing Inn next week. And I want that more than anything else in the world.

With closed eyes and a quiet hum, I find my pitch. All the chattering sounds of my classmates go silent as I focus on the words I need to sing. The raw and thrilling excitement I get at the start of every challenge I've ever faced races through my veins.

Then my sister's voice pops my focus.

"You got this!" she whisper-screams. My eyes fly open. Okalee Luz Petersen, my ten-year-old sister, is in the front row.

Parents aren't supposed to have a favorite child, but mine do, and she's sitting right there in front of me, a huge grin on her face, her skinny thumbs bouncing up and down like she just can't contain them. Okalee earns straight As. She's got bony arms and legs, but she tries her best in PE, dashing toward opponents during winter basketball or launching herself into the air to catch a football in the spring. Her science experiments are at the level of an eighth grader, and she wins blue ribbons at the science fair every year. Her teacher, Mrs. Dixon, always posts her poems, her artwork, and even her math assignments on the brag board in the hallway.

I've never made it onto that board.

My two best friends, Wardie Mason and Helena McClain, sit on either side of Okalee. Helena nods in her calm way. *You'll be great*, she mouths.

Wardie's smile is tight. He's nervous for me—a concept Okalee doesn't understand.

"Ready?" Ms. Loring says, fingers poised over the baby grand.

"You're the best singer ever!" Okalee says, still whisper-screaming, and I can't help but smile. I also can't help but look at Kat Waters to see if she heard. Kat's standing right below the stage. Her arms are crossed tight across her chest. She's chewing gum so fast I can see her jaw pounding at the inside of her cheek. It's like the gum is crying, "Help! I'm sick of being chewed! Get me out of this crazy girl!"

"I still don't get why we're holding an audition," says Lucia, Kat's right-hand minion, parroting Kat's usual audition speech right back at her. "We all know *you're* the best singer ever, Kat."

Kat tosses her a sharp "Shut up!" and then catches herself, smiling at Ms. Loring. Ms. Loring frowns. She's no Mrs. Butters, that's for sure. Our old music teacher never could resist Kat's sugary manipulations. That's why Kat has sung the solo for almost every single Grayling Crossing Elementary School concert since we were in the first grade—Christmas, Annual Spring, Alumni Weekend— you name it, she got it.

Well, *almost* every single concert. In the second grade, Kat forgot to sprinkle her meanness with sugar, and she yelled at Mrs. Butters to play the piano slower during the Christmas program auditions, so I won the solo for "Mary, Did You Know?" But that was just a cute performance in the lower-grade choir.

Now I'm in the middle-school choir, the serious one, and my voice has changed. It can soar higher, loop deeper, hold notes longer than before.

Mrs. Butters always gave me a B+ in music. Music is my best subject, and I want a shining grade in it. My grades are two Ds, three Cs, and one B.

I'm desperate for an A.

Now that Ms. Loring is in charge, I have a real chance to get the solo and finally earn one. Singing makes me feel alive and free. Good at something people care about. If I can't make a living climbing trees and jumping off bridges into clear summertime rivers, then I want to make a living by singing. If I told Mamá and Dad that, they'd tell me how hard it is to support yourself as a musician. So I keep it to myself.

They don't understand how good I am at it. How much I love it. They're always too busy praising Okalee or lecturing me about my grades.

Ms. Loring told us that whoever earns the solo will not only benefit extremely from the musical experience of polishing and performing a major solo but will also earn an A grade for the third quarter of school, which ends right after the concert.

If I can show Mamá and Dad an A in music on my report card, maybe they won't send me to summer school in Bozeman. The thought of spending my days locked in a cinder-block school while summer waits for me just outside the window makes me tremble.

"Phoebe?" Ms. Loring says again. "Just nod when you're ready."

I close my eyes again for focus. I've watched the YouTube video of a serious-looking Alison Krauss singing "Down in the River to Pray" a thousand times. I thought and thought about how I could add my own flair to it. I've spent countless afternoons locked in the basement bathroom with my eyes closed, singing the solo over and over, listening to my voice swirl and echo in the tiny space. It always sounded beautiful in there, each day a little better than before.

Our school is a tiny country elementary where everybody has to sing in the choir or else a choir would not exist, so I'm about to sing in front of the whole school. Not alone in a bathroom with perfect acoustics.

I open my eyes. The kindergarteners and first-graders wiggle in their seats. A girl in Okalee's class passes a note over a row to a girl in the third grade. Two of my classmates are playing volleyball with an empty plastic water bottle. When I left my seat to come up to the stage, Okalee snuck to my spot in the first row, where my whole sixth-grade class is sitting, for moral support. A few teachers tried to shoo her back to her correct seat, but she ignored them. Okalee has a stubborn streak when she wants to. She's sitting between Wardie and Helena, and her excitement is a spotlight shining right on her tight yellow curls. Thankfully, Ms. Loring doesn't seem to mind.

I shift on the stage, take a breath so deep it echoes in the microphone. I think of the sweet summer days that can be mine if I win this: mornings rafting the Grayling River on inner tubes with Wardie, buttered tortillas rolled up in our hands. Not the dry grocery store ones but his mami's soft, moist, homemade ones. Afternoons spent riding horses at Helena's family ranch, The Lazy M. Cool evenings walking along the riverbank with Okalee and Mamá and Dad, listening to the rattling call of a blue-black kingfisher and the watery trill of a red-winged blackbird.

And I think of Dad and Mamá's faces when they hear me sing in front of everyone. Mamá will dab tears from her eyes, and Dad will beam with surprised pride. I won't be the old Phoebe who's as strong and tough as a big, hairy ox. I won't be the old Phoebe that everyone thinks needs extra tutoring.

I'll be a new Phoebe they never saw before: Phoebe with the singing voice that can stir even the coldest heart to life. And they'll wonder how they could have failed to see my gift through all these years.

Ms. Loring snaps her fingers at the kids playing water-bottle volleyball. "Enough," she says firmly. She locks eyes with me. I nod for her to play the introduction, and the piano swallows the sounds of chatter and laughter and the crackling water bottle.

I open my mouth and imagine that my throat is a valley between two mountains. My voice reaches to the valley floor, scooping a deep alto from among the grasses there, and then I set it free.

> *As I went down in the river to pray,*
> *Studying about that good old way*
> *And who shall wear the starry crown*
> *Good Lord, show me the way.*

The air in the gym shifts.
No one's whispering. No one's wiggling.

> *O sisters, let's go down*
> *Let's go down, come on down*
> *O sisters, let's go down*
> *Down in the river to pray.*

My voice gets louder and stronger. A feeling like the first aspen leaves turning sunshine-yellow in the fall or the Grayling River melting in spring trickles through me. A smile blooms on my face as I let the notes and the words reach their fingers into the gym and clasp the hands of anyone willing to hold on.

> *O brothers, let's go down*
> *Let's go down, come on down*
> *Come on, brothers, let's go down*
> *Down in the river to pray.*

I hold the last note for a moment, and then, reluctantly, I draw my voice back into my chest.

Before I'm done reclaiming my breath, a loud cheer bursts through the gym, and it's coming from all my classmates. Ms. Loring grins at me. Wardie and Okalee are hopping up and down and yelling.

"That was awesome!" Helena shouts. I sprint down the stage steps, tripping and landing hard on the wooden gym floor. Pain ripples into my arm, my hip, my leg.

But I'm laughing. I did it. I sang better than I ever have in my life, and it made me feel like a bird perched in the top of a spruce tree, song springing from its lungs.

"Phoebe!" Wardie helps me stand. "Are you okay? That was epic." Quieter, he says, "Ms. Loring'll do the right thing. She'll give the solo to you."

My cheeks burn. I hope he's right. We sit back down, and I huddle so close to Okalee that we're practically sitting on the same chair.

Okalee leans into me as Ms. Loring motions the last student onto the stage. It's Kat, and she's not smiling.

"That was awesome, Phoebe," Okalee whispers.

I cuddle into her. She smells like dandelions and toothpaste and pride. "I hope Kat messes up."

"That's mean." Okalee swats at me. "'Do unto others,' Phoebe."

I groan. Okalee has taken it upon herself to read the Bible every Sunday, since we don't go to church except for Easter Sunday and Christmas Eve, and she feels the need to "explore Jesus's ways and be a shining ray of his light," as she put it to Mamá this morning. She says that as a pediatric nurse—which is what she wants to be when she grows up—she has to be like Jesus, kind and healing and like a warm swallow of soup on a winter day. I don't know how she knows that Jesus is like soup, but I do know that her holiness makes me feel like sinning.

Before I can think of a good comeback for Okalee, Kat begins to sing.

I watch her carefully, studying the long O her mouth makes as it moves over the words. I'll admit it: she sounds good, like an opera singer. Her blonde hair swishes at her chin with each soprano note, her chin doubling at the alto ones. She's even holding her hands in a dainty clasp just above her rib cage.

As she sings the final words, she looks right at me. Her

eyes are the blazing cloudless blue of a day that knows it's beautiful. *I bet I just won the solo*, they say.

I make myself clap for her, holding her stare until she looks away, smiling confidently at Ms. Loring.

Okalee pats my leg. "Way to be a good sport."

But I'm not clapping because of that. I'm clapping to smash my anxiousness between my hands like it's a slice of plantain for one of Mamá's famous tostones.

Ms. Loring nods at Kat. "Your voice has a beautiful tone," she says.

Kat shoots me a triumphant glance.

Ms. Loring asks Kat to take a seat and then clickety-clacks onto the stage. She bends her long neck to speak in the microphone.

She clears her throat. "I want to thank the teachers for taking the time out of class to bring your students to this extended practice and audition for the twenty-fifth annual Spring Concert, and I'd also like to thank each of you brave souls who auditioned. There's nothing quite as scary and thrilling as singing on a stage in front of a crowd."

"I almost barfed," pipes Gracie Henry, a first-grader with a sweet, clear voice. Everyone laughs.

"I'm glad you didn't, Gracie." Ms. Loring smiles. "I'll first announce the soloist for 'Inchworm,' which our lower-grade choir will be performing at the concert. It was very close, kids. So close that I have decided to split the solo in half and give it to the two students I could not decide between. Drumroll, please."

An excited pitter-pat of hands slapping thighs fills the gym. I make myself do it, too, even though I want Ms. Loring to get it over with already and announce the middle-school soloist.

"And our soloists are . . . Benny Ripwinkle and Gracie Henry!" Cheers rise. Ms. Loring steps off the stage to congratulate the winners.

Okalee says, "Yay, Gracie!" Then she grabs both my hands. "Here we go, Phoebe. It's gotta be you, it's gotta be you, it's gotta be you."

"But if it's not, remember that you're still the best singer I've ever heard," Helena says. "And someday, everyone will know it."

I don't tell her that I feel like it's now or never. If Ms. Loring chooses Kat, it means Kat really can sing better than I can.

"She's going back on stage," Wardie says, and we stop talking.

"Can I have everyone's attention?" Ms. Loring clasps the microphone stand with one hand and smooths her pinstripe skirt with the other. "Our soloist for 'Down in the River to Pray' was also very tough to decide, but once all the solos had been sung, I knew in my heart who would fill that spot best."

My teacher, Mr. Ripwinkle, snorts, probably at Ms. Loring's flowery language, which I happen to like.

"Another drumroll, yes?" she says. "But this time let's use our feet!"

Stomping thunders through the gym. I can almost feel Kat's anticipation pulsing through the metal chairs from her end of the row to mine. I squeeze my knees together and curl my body on top of them like I'm protecting myself from a charging grizzly.

Please please please.

"And our soloist is . . ."

I stop breathing.

"Phoebe Petersen!"

I take a deep, gasping breath and sit up straight as though I've just broken through the surface of a glacial lake. "Did she just say Phoebe? Did she just say me?"

"She said Phoebe!" Okalee shrieks. "You did it! You won!"

Helena hugs me, her face crinkled into a satisfied, cheesy smile.

Wardie grabs my shoulders and gives them a happy shake. "I knew it," he says. "I knew Ms. Loring would do the right thing."

I laugh. And once I start, I can't stop. Then a chair screaks on the gym floor, and Kat rises, hands fisted at her sides.

"It can't be," she says. The loud chatter rushes on, but her words bang around in my head. "You've made a mistake," she says again, louder this time. "Right?"

Mr. Ripwinkle looks at her, amused. Ms. Loring turns toward Kat.

"I'm sorry, Katherine," she says. "You have a wonderful voice too—and to be honest, you were my second choice—but I feel in this case that Phoebe—"

"You don't understand. I always sing the solos."

The whole gym goes silent. Ms. Loring blinks. "Maybe so, but not this time, Kat," she says slowly. "Now, please. If you'd like to talk about this in private, I'd be—"

"There's a scout coming," Kat says, her voice desperate. "The director of the travel choir for Bozeman High is coming to listen to me sing. I was supposed to sing my solo for him. Hundreds audition, but only a few people get in, don't you see? If he likes what he hears, he'll hold a spot for me."

"I wonder how much her dad paid the guy for *that*," Helena mutters.

Ms. Loring shakes her head. "Kat, sweetie—"

"I am not your sweetie!" Kat snaps.

Okalee gasps. Blotches of red creep up Ms. Loring's neck. She looks younger than her twenty-two years all of a sudden, and she's blinking really fast like she might cry.

I would, too, if Kat humiliated me in front of everybody like that.

I stand up, step out of the row of sixth-graders, and face Kat.

Now what? Should I say, *Ms. Loring's the teacher, not you?* No, that will only make her madder at Ms. Loring. *You did a great job, Kat, I'm sure you'll get it next time?* Yuck, no. I am not Okalee. I think of Mrs. Butters's cowed look each time she announced Kat the winner of a solo, of honest Ms. Loring's humiliation now.

And then I know what to say.

"We've gotten to hear your amazing voice at so many concerts over the years, Kat," I say, letting what I hope is a buttery smile grace my face. "But this time the audition was fair and square."

"Oh snap," Wardie says. Someone else giggles.

Kat's mouth pinches shut. Her eyes bulge.

I turn to Ms. Loring and fold my hands together to keep them from shaking. I know I will pay for this later. "I would be honored to sing the solo, Ms. Loring."

She nods, leans into the microphone, and says, with forced brightness, "The concert is in just over a week, everybody, so soloists and choir members alike, remember to come to class with a good attitude, ready to work. And try not to eat too much dairy on choir days, because it can cause phlegm."

"We don't want anyone hocking loogies in class," Mr. Ripwinkle adds quietly with a laugh.

Giggles spring from the lower-grade rows.

Ms. Loring grins. "Class is dismissed."

Mr. Ripwinkle faces our class. Kat starts elbowing toward me, but he holds a hand out to her. "Save your dramatics for later, Katherine. Class, please be at your desks and ready for school dismissal in five minutes."

Just as I'm sliding out the door, listening to words of congratulations from my classmates and even from some of the seventh- and eighth-graders, someone grabs my arm, fingernails digging into my bare flesh.

"Ow!" I whip around and come face-to-face with Kat. Tears quiver on her eyelashes. I pry her fingers off my arm. "What do you want?"

"Please give me the solo, Phoebe. I'll give you anything. I'll give you fifty dollars, if you want. Seventy-five?"

"I don't want money."

"A hundred, then."

"Kat. I don't want your money."

She shakes her head in teeny, tiny motions like she's searching for another angle. And when she spits out the words, they shake me more than I let myself show.

"I'll do your homework, then. You know I could get you As in math. Aren't you failing that? And science too?"

That is none of your business! I want to scream. But I

say, "Stop begging me for the solo. It's not like Ms. Loring would let me give it to you anyway."

A tear tracks down her cheek. She swipes it away, furious. She checks over her shoulder and then whispers, voice tight, "I'll get it from you. You better watch out."

2

I grab Okalee's hand right after dismissal. The Gallatin Valley opens wide outside the front doors, flat fields leading to distant mountains. Okalee and I walk into the small field behind the school, and I gaze up at the mountains, the ones that hug our town in a jagged curve. They're so close I can see each fir tree individually. Each dark-green limb is a possible point to climb, to see out over the valley and the river.

Nothing steals my breath away like the sight of those mountains. Dad always says how lucky we are to live in this town huddled below them, and he's right. Grayling Crossing is the last stop before you drive into the mountains where some of the big ski resorts are, where Dad works construction and maintenance jobs all year long: Big Sky. The Yellowstone Club. There's endless space for

Wardie, Helena, Okalee, and me to run and climb and explore.

You'd think life would be quiet here with the town's population of 968, give or take a few, but we all know each other a little too well. Still, I love it. Mamá works in Bozeman, and sometimes she takes us to see a play, concert, or poetry reading at the university when we need to get away. Sometimes we escape the smallness of our town by heading to Costco in Bozeman for a load of oversized everything.

Here, in Grayling Crossing, we have just one small grocery store, a couple of coffee shops and restaurants, a post office, a school, and the Grayling River, which runs past the outer edge of town and toward the foothills of the mountains. The elementary school and the one muddy wheat field behind it divides the river from the town. Some things—like the mountains, the fir and aspen forests, my spread-out neighborhood, and the river—are behind the school. Other, larger plots of land, like Helena's family's ranch, are on the town side of the river, the flatter side near the main road that leads to Bozeman.

As Okalee and I walk, we pass Bo, Helena's Appaloosa, who's tied to a post between the playground and the soccer field. This year, she got special permission to ride him the three miles to school from her family's ranch. The flat soccer field gives way to the small wheat field that one of my classmates' parents owns. All of us who live along the Grayling River walk through this field to get home, and our footsteps have carved a trail that leads to the Oxtail Bridge.

All Okalee and I have to do is cross the Oxtail and we're home. Wardie's house is right next to the bridge. Sometimes, right before we cross it, we look over and see Mrs. Mason waving at us from her dining room window.

I speed up. Black, sucking mud squelches beneath my shoes.

"Why are you walking so fast?" Okalee's cold fingers squeeze mine. "Slow down, Phoebe."

I keep walking, the stiff spring wind pushing me forward.

"You won. Aren't you excited?"

"Kat said she's going to steal the solo."

Okalee snorts. "She can't do that." Her voice softens. "She's really sad is all. She wishes she'd won."

I don't say anything. Kat's always had this power at school, not only over Mrs. Butters but also over Ms. Ames, Mrs. Dixon, Mr. Piper—all our teachers until Mr. Ripwinkle and Ms. Loring.

I slow my step finally and tell Okalee, "I'm just annoyed with Kat, Okie. She *had* to make a scene during the most awesome moment of my life so far."

"It's *Okalee*," she insists. "Unless you want to be *Pheebs*."

A laugh builds in my chest and spills out over the field, releasing some of my annoyance with Kat. "I won the solo, Okalee. I really won it."

"And Kat Waters can't do anything about it, no matter how mad she gets," Okalee says. She looks over her shoulder. "Plus there's something I have to tell you."

"What's that?" I feel lighter already. Okalee's right. Kat can threaten all she wants, but she can't actually take my solo from me.

Okalee lowers her voice. "I heard Mamá and Dad talking last night, saying they're gonna go visit Great-Aunt Astrid tomorrow morning."

I stop walking. Our parents used to make us come with them to visit Great-Aunt Astrid, but since I started middle school, they let Okalee and me stay home alone. Great-Aunt Astrid lives in a nursing home fifteen minutes away in Bozeman, but Mamá and Dad always stay for several hours when they go because they usually only see her once or twice a month.

Okalee's face is eager.

"And the ice is all melted from the river," I say. I'd noticed when I crossed the Oxtail Bridge that morning.

A red-winged blackbird trills from somewhere in the

aspens ahead of us, and my heart lifts with the song. *River Day*.

There are two things in this world that I can do better than Okalee: sing and swim.

I invented River Day when I was nine and Okalee was seven. It's a secret just between us—a celebration of spring. Every March or April, depending on how fast the ice is melting, we slip out of the house while our parents are sleeping and go down to the river. I hold Okalee's hand tight, and we cross the river, step by rocky step. Then we sneak back into the house, burying our wet swimsuits in the bottom of our laundry baskets.

Each year, we cross a little earlier in the season than the year before, even though there's an unspoken rule in the neighborhood that all the kids who live along the river aren't supposed to go in until June. But together Okalee and I make a fearless team. Sometimes Okalee keeps me strong, like when I'm worried about Kat or I'm about to take a math test. But out in the forests and rivers, I'm the one who keeps her strong. River Day is my favorite of our sister adventures because I'm a good swimmer. We always hold hands tight, and I always make sure Okalee gets across safely.

Now, for the first time, we have the chance to cross when Mamá and Dad aren't at home. That means we can get up a little later, like at eight o'clock when it's a touch warmer out, and there'll be no chance of them catching us.

"You're right," I say softly, looking over my shoulder to make sure Wardie's not within earshot. He told me earlier he'd be staying after school with David Carter to study for our upcoming science test, but I have to make sure Okalee and I are alone. I can't risk anyone hearing about River Day.

Wardie wants to be a park ranger when he grows up. He's working hard at school so he can do well in the environmental biology program at Montana State University. In the winter, he uses a chisel and a tape measure to check the river ice so he knows that we're skating on at least four solid inches. The moment it starts thinning out, he and I stay off the river, and from then on, he firmly backs the no-river-until-June rule that all the riverbank parents have.

He'd make his father, who's a police officer, lock me up if he knew about River Day.

A hawk's wobbly *scree* twists in the air. The dark, damp smell of mud climbs into my nose. A breeze presses its cool breath on my shoulders and spills down the back of my blouse. River Day always reminds me that I am capable. I am powerful.

I think of how it felt, singing the solo today. Kat's anger can't follow me through the Grayling River. I'll emerge on the other side triumphant, ready to battle anything Kat might send my way.

Okalee grins. "Tomorrow is River Day, sister." Then her lips straighten in determination. She stands tall. "I'm going to cross without holding your hand this year. I've been practicing, and my swimming is just as good as yours now."

"*No.*" I whirl around.

"But—"

"I said no. You have to promise me you won't go in without me. If you don't promise, we won't do River Day this year."

Okalee crosses her arms. "Oh, come on."

"I'm dead serious." I stop in front of Okalee and stand as tall as I can. I cross my arms, muscular from climbing so many trees. I straighten my strong shoulders. River Day is more than just an adventure. It's a challenge that Okalee and I can only conquer if we do it hand in hand.

"Please, Phoebe, I—"

"Promise me. No promise, no River Day."

Okalee sighs dramatically. "Fine, I promise."

I stick my pinkie out, and she slowly worms hers around mine. We lock pinkies, and I look straight into her brown eyes to show her that I'm the most serious person in the world right now.

She nods slightly. "Tomorrow is River Day, and I promise we'll cross together." She spins away and runs ahead of me across the bridge.

Our house sits on the bank of the Grayling River, right

across the river from the Masons' house. Or the Mason-Marín house, as Mamá and Mrs. Mason say. They both changed their names when they got married, but they still put their maiden names at the end of their married names. Unofficially, but still kind of official. Like a little reminder that just because they got married, it doesn't mean they aren't the women they were before.

In my mind, their names are like this: *Soledad Peterson (Santos). Dulce Mason (Marín).* They both say that in Cuba, where Mamá's from, or in México, where Mrs. Mason is from, they would've kept the names they grew up with. But they both married American men who didn't really get it. So to fit in, they changed their names. Kind of like Wardie did; his real name is Eduardo. He says that when kids at school tried to pronounce it, it sounded all drawn-out and twangy. He hated it. So instead, he's Wardie. Only his mami calls him Eduardo.

The Oxtail Bridge opens up into the canopy of evergreens that line my front yard. I'm just stepping into the trees when Bo's hooves clatter onto the bridge. Helena's house is in the opposite direction from mine.

"Phoebe!" Helena calls. "Come here for a sec."

We meet at the mouth of the bridge, where Helena dismounts and leads Bo down to the riverbank.

"What?" My voice comes out more impatient than I want it to, but I'm bursting to tell Mamá about my solo.

"Hang on just a second." Helena paws through her backpack. While I wait, I stroke Bo's apple of a cheek, my fingers dancing over the soft hair on his muzzle.

"Aha!" Helena tugs a folded piece of paper out of her backpack. "I didn't want to give it to you before the audition in case it made you more nervous. But I really think you could do it."

Helena's eyes are like a fire snapping in a woodstove on a below-zero morning.

"Open it," she says.

I unfold the paper, and the bird that was trapped in my chest earlier starts flapping its wings again.

-AMERICA'S VOICE-
BOZEMAN EDITION

DO YOU HAVE BOZEMAN'S NEXT STUNNING NEW VOICE?
DO YOU DREAM OF SINGING FOR CROWDS OF THOUSANDS?

Then come to the Gallatin Valley Mall on April 7 at 4 pm to dazzle our judges with your talent! Three winners will be chosen, but first place gets a Golden Ticket to the America's Voice Season 7 auditions in Los Angeles, California, held on May 16!

(Airfare and three nights in an area hotel included. One guest also paid for.)

BEST OF LUCK TO EVERYONE WHO AUDITIONS!

Note: All singers must provide their own accompaniment. A piano will be provided. All other instruments must be brought.

I hold the paper so tight my fingernails turn white. *America's Voice.* Mamá, Dad, Okalee, and I watch it every Wednesday night with the Masons, sometimes at our house and sometimes at theirs. Always, we eat our favorite Cuban and Mexican foods while we watch: chips with Mrs. Mason's fresh salsa or Mamá's creamy-sweet homemade flan. Here in Montana, we're some of the only Latine people around. *Tenemos que stick together*, Dad always says in his perfect Spanglish.

Four judges critique the contestants' singing performances, and then the audience texts in votes for which singer should win that night's competition. Whoever has the fewest votes goes home. When only two contestants remain, they each put on their best show, dazzling audiences with everything they've learned about singing over the past weeks. And then one of them, chosen again by America, wins a record deal with a big label and a management contract with judge Sergio Fabrizi's well-respected company.

In other words, if I audition in Bozeman and win the Golden Ticket, I wouldn't have to worry about bad grades anymore. I would stay in school, but only because I had to. Mamá and Dad wouldn't be able to hound me so much about studying and tutoring and summer school and getting into a good college. They wouldn't have to worry about my future because I'd be a famous singer.

They'd be proud.

"Well?" Helena steps close. "Are you gonna do it?"

I imagine standing on the stage in front of the judges with my hair done up nice and my tan skin sweaty with nerves and hope.

The answer is clear.

"I'll do it," I say. "But don't tell anybody. I don't want anybody to know until the second I get on stage at the mall."

I don't want someone like Kat to find out about this, which she probably will, but the later the better. The *America's Voice* audition will be my secret. I imagine how surprised everyone would be when I step onto that stage. I shiver with delight.

"I knew you'd do it!" Helena wraps her arms around me, her faint hay smell as comforting as a cup of tea. "You'll win it. You'll get to go to Los Angeles for the real thing. I just have this feeling."

And because Helena's almost always right about things, I let myself believe that she could be right this time too.

⟡

I fly through the mudroom and into the kitchen. Mamá's leaning against the counter, one arm wrapped around the big, yellow mixing bowl, the other stirring the dough inside. She's whistling a jazzy tune she made up long before I was born; the sound of it always makes me feel light and free.

"Sorry I'm late." I whip my apron on and take out the cookie sheet.

"You look excited about something." Mamá hands me the bowl. The dough inside matches the chipped enamel on the outside.

I look up. "Lemon cookies?"

"Yes!" Okalee says from the table, where she's already buried in a heap of homework.

"Sí, limón." Mamá rests her hands on either side of the sink and smiles out the window. Her curls, corkscrew-tight like Okalee's but dark like my wavy hair, spill out of the clip she pinned them back with this morning. "La primavera viene, mija. Lemon is perfect for this weather." She turns to me. "How was school?" There's a faint *eh* attached to the beginning of the word *school*, a trace of the Cuban accent she left behind when her family fled Fidel Castro's regime in the eighties.

I take a spoon and start scooping the cookie dough onto the sheet. "I have news, Mamá."

"Oh?" Mamá's eyes light up. "Cuéntame."

It's hard to hold my smile back. "I won the lead choir solo for the twenty-fifth annual Spring Concert at the Grayling Crossing Inn next week!"

A grin breaks out on her face. "That's wonderful!" She

takes my chin in her hands, and the Band-Aid wrapped around her finger feels rough on my skin. She works part-time at Sew Sweet, and she almost always has a bandage wrapped around whatever finger she pricked that day.

Mamá kisses my cheek. "I'm proud, hija. We haven't heard that beautiful voice of yours sing from a stage in too long." Then she tilts her head and asks the question I knew she'd ask. "Will it improve your grade in the class?"

I nod, batting away a twinge of annoyance.

She crosses her arms and scoots closer to me so that the hems of our aprons touch. Mine is blue and green like the Grayling in the summertime, with a ruffled hem that reminds me of a surging current. Mamá's is red with a lace hem. She made them herself and surprised me with mine last Christmas. Okalee didn't get one because Okalee doesn't bake with Mamá every day after school like I do.

Mamá takes a tiny cup of dark, foamy coffee—Cuban coffee—and sips at it. She closes her eyes.

"Can I have some?" I love Cuban coffee, which is the only type of coffee Mamá will drink, but she rarely lets me have it. It has way more caffeine than American coffee. Today, though, she lets me take a sip. The foam tickles my lip. The strong, sweet, thick brew slides over my tongue. I close my eyes too.

"I could drink a whole cup of that," I say, grinning at Mamá.

She whisks it away. "Quick, get those cookies in the oven so you can start your homework," she says, leaning her shoulder into mine.

I rest my head on her warm, plump shoulder and frown. She doesn't usually rush me like this. We have an agreement: while the cookies are in the oven, I can step outside and breathe the fresh air and gaze at the river and listen to the birdsong. But when the cookies finish baking, I've got to go in and start my homework. Homework is less cruel with a sugary treat melting on my tongue.

"But I thought—"

"Phoebe." Mamá stands up straight. She holds me by the shoulders and nods at Okalee, and I know exactly what that means. *Be a little more like your sister today, okay?*

I look at Okalee's golden head bent over her spelling book. She glances up and smiles at me.

I smile back.

"Phoebe? ¿Me oíste?" Mamá says.

"Sí, Mamá." I slide the cookie sheet into the oven and try to summon up some joy at the thought of eating a tangy lemon cookie in ten minutes. But I feel droopy now.

The chance of an A has made Mamá too hopeful about the rest of my grades.

3

Early the next morning, my door creaks open. For an instant, my heart thumps wildly. But then the familiar slope of Dad's shoulders registers in my brain through the soupy light of dawn.

He sits on the edge of my bed, all 240 pounds of him weighing on it so that my feet slide down the side.

"Hey," he says quietly. "You awake?"

I nod.

"We're leaving for Great-Aunt Astrid's," he says. "She says she has a story from her girlhood in Norway to tell me. Something about her and my mother hiding in an old stave church and scaring tourists." He smiles.

In all Great-Aunt Astrid's stories, she and Dad's mother, my Mormor Ida, who died of cancer when I was five, were known in their village as the most mischievous and adventurous sisters around. A little bit like Okalee and me.

"Anyway," Dad says, "we'll be back sometime after lunch." He shifts and runs a hand over the stubble on his face. His smile turns serious. "Phoebe, I'm proud of you. Mamá told me about your solo." He'd gotten back late last night from his job overseeing the building of some rich person's house near Big Sky Resort, and I'd already gone to bed.

He runs his fingers through my hair. "I just wanted to tell you that before we go. Your mom and I are very hopeful that this is a turning point for you," he says haltingly, like maybe he didn't think of the words himself, like maybe Mamá asked him to say this to me.

I'm wide awake now. Frustration wells up in me. Why can't the promise of an A in music be enough for them? I squeeze the edges of my quilt. "I'm not Okalee," I say. "Don't expect too much."

Dad raises his eyebrows. "Oh, Phoebe." He leans in and kisses my forehead, the scratch of his beard the most familiar thing in the world. "I shouldn't have said that. We know you try your hardest, and we can't wait to hear you sing."

I burrow into him.

"Take good care of your sister today," he says, easing himself off the edge of the bed.

"I will, Daddy."

The door clicks shut. I lie there thinking about how to make my solo sound so stunning that Mamá and Dad forget all about my other grades. A little while later the 4Runner rumbles away, toward Great-Aunt Astrid and her Norway stories.

⸱

An hour later, Okalee and I stand at the edge of the Grayling River. Okalee's wearing her yellow swimsuit, but I couldn't find mine, so I have on shorts and a tank top. The air smells sweet, muddy, hopeful. Even facing the brown, rushing river makes me feel powerful; I can already see Kat's anger and Mamá and Dad's doubts drowning in these waters. The pebbles of the riverbank send thrills of cold into my bare feet. No lights are on in Wardie's log house across the river or in any of the houses scattered farther up and downriver, though they're far enough from here that you couldn't see us crossing. At least not very clearly, unless you had binoculars.

A bobbing movement in the spruces upriver catches my eye. Then it disappears. I squint, but I don't see the movement again. Probably just a deer running on a path the animals have carved through the forest.

I dip my toe into the water and inhale sharply. This river is only a few breaths away from icy, and it seems louder and angrier than it did yesterday. In another couple of weeks, the snowmelt will slow down. But Mamá and Dad are gone, and today's a perfect day, sunny and creeping up on warm.

And it's not River Day if the river's not tough to cross.

Okalee's watching the river, curls dancing in the morning breeze.

"Okalee? Remember your promise?"

"I keep my promises, Phoebe." She faces me. "Just let me know when you're ready."

I start to reach for her hand, but just then a blackbird trills from the reeds to the left of us. Okalee turns and points. "Look," she whispers.

Two red-winged blackbirds perch on a set of cattails.

O-ka-lee! O-ka-lee!

I smile at them. The ruby patches on their wings flash in the morning sun. Dad named my sister after these bold, loud birds and their trilling call. He loves birds—our whole family does—and sometimes I wish he'd named my sister Finch or Dove. But he had to call her Okalee, our blackbird, sleek as midnight and feisty as that flash of ruby red.

A quiet splash jerks me out of my thoughts. I turn back to the river and freeze with horror.

Okalee is in the water. I stare openmouthed at the current licking her ankles.

She takes another step. The river swallows her ankles and starts to climb her calves, and I snap back to my senses.

"Hey!" She's only a few feet away from me, so I jump into the river and grab her elbow. "What are you doing? You promised."

"Let go of me." She tries to pry my fingers off her arm, but I squeeze tight. "I crossed my fingers behind my back yesterday, so it wasn't a real promise."

"You've got to be kidding me," I say. "That's the stupidest thing I ever heard."

Okalee snorts. "I'll be fine. I'm stronger than you think, Phoebe." She tugs. I clamp tighter. "You're hurting me. Let me go! You started River Day when you were younger than I am now. I can cross without you."

"I'm stronger than you, and I know this river way better than you do. You promised you would cross with me. You *promised*." Last year, Okalee clamped my hand so hard she could barely open hers after we were done.

With a grunt, Okalee rips her hand out of mine. "I'm strong too," she says with a proud look on her face. She shakes her fingers out hard. "And I know the river. It's wet and cold and not in charge of me." *Just like you're not*, her eyes say.

I want to shout, *I am in charge of you! Dad told me to take care of you.* But I keep the words locked behind my teeth. If I say them, headstrong Okalee will plow deeper into the river.

I try something different. "You're being sassy and

stubborn, Okalee. What happened to the what-would-Jesus-do thing?"

For a moment, she freezes. Her eyelid twitches. Then she straightens and says, "Jesus would stand up for himself, like I am. He'd want you to believe in what I can do. He believed Peter could walk on water."

"You are not Peter, and Jesus is not here to make a miracle out of you!" I snap. "You've got to listen to me. You're only a little—"

I stop.

"Little what?" Okalee's hands jam into her hips.

The sun glares off the water. Okalee has ruined River Day. "Get out of the water," I say, channeling my inner Mamá. "We're going back inside."

She doesn't move. "What were you gonna say, Phoebe?"

She knows. I can't lie to her.

I dig my heels into the sharp pebbles of the riverbed. "You're just a little kid, that's what I was going to say. You're not big enough to cross alone—not strong enough—"

Okalee's mouth bunches into a tight knot. She wipes her hands on her bare legs and glares at me. "I might be littler than *you*, but I am not a little kid. Just like I'm smarter than you, but we all know you're not stupid."

I'm stunned by her sharp words. Yes, she's smart. Really smart and bright and perfect. But I can outshine Okalee in other ways, right? She's standing there with flashing eyes and hands on her hips and golden curls flying, and next to her, I feel like a frumpy, brown-haired, dull, responsible party pooper.

Before I can catch my breath or think of a comeback, Okalee whirls toward the churning water. Her thin shoulder blades push against her swimsuit.

Party pooper or not, I can't let her go in that river alone. "Seriously, Okalee, you have to hold my hand, or else we go inside right now." I grab for her elbow, but she wrenches her arm away so hard she twists and falls forward. Her chin skims the river water, but she catches herself and stands up straight.

"Don't shove me!"

Frustration swells in my chest. "I wasn't trying to shove you. You have to hold my hand or you *cannot* cross." I reach for her again, but she barges deeper into the water.

"Yes, I can," she calls over her shoulder. "Watch me."

The cold water of the Grayling stiffens her arms and squeezes her hands into fists. She wades fast, farther and farther into the muddy current. The river swallows her legs and dances around her waist. I can't look away, and I can't move either.

She's really doing it. She's crossing by herself.

Then panic coils around my throat. The riverbank parents have a June rule for a reason, and that reason is clear right now: the river is big and brown and loud. What we're doing right now goes against everything our parents have taught us about river safety. It goes against everything we know is right. I never cared about that before because I knew that if Okalee and I crossed together, we'd be fine. We always were.

"Don't go another step," I yell. "I'm coming to help you."

The river roars. She doesn't turn around. I can't tell if she's ignoring me or if she can't hear me.

She takes another step. The river licks her skinny chest.

I leap toward the middle of the river and lunge, lunge, lunge. The water slaps my chest and I gasp; it's so cold. My legs push hard against the murky current. "Okalee, please. Just let me help you."

Okalee keeps crossing, step by step.

She reaches the middle of the river, her hands sifting the water to find the boulder that marks the halfway point.

The boulder. Where's the boulder?

A rock stabs my foot. The snow in the mountains must be melting faster than I thought, because the river has swallowed all but the boulder's very tip. Last year on River Day, it stood almost halfway out of the water.

"Okalee, stay there," I scream.

Okalee turns. Her hands are still under the current, holding on to the rock's slick surface. Her face is wet and determined. Her mocking lips say, "Halfway!"

"Stop!" I wave my arms. I'm fifteen feet from her at most.

The current yanks at my legs, and I tighten my stomach muscles to steady myself. I'm amazed that Okalee, skinny Okalee, made it as far as she did.

Okalee squints. She looks worried now, scared, but still determined.

"No, Okalee. Don't leave the rock."

But she can't hear me. She takes a step, fumbles, and falls.

The river drags her surprised eyes under its brown surface. For one moment, I see the golden tips of her curls before they vanish.

The sight snatches all the air out of my lungs. I have to force myself to take a gasping breath before diving underwater. I claw at the riverbed's pebbles and silt and push my eyes open, but all I see is mud. The river twists my arms and shoves my legs.

I bend my knees and use the riverbed to jump-swim my way to air again. I look for a hand or a foot or any part of Okalee sticking out of the current.

Then her face surfaces.

She's four feet from me.

One arm reaches for me, fingers clawed.

"Okalee!"

4

I'm under the Oxtail Bridge. I swam and ran and ended up here, looking looking looking after—

No. Don't think of that.

My breath comes in shallow bursts. I slump against the boulders and cement that support the bridge's frame. Dirt fills my eyes, nostrils, mouth. I swipe my face to see better, but the Grayling's surface is unbroken.

A red-winged blackbird perches on the bridge's railing, its dark eyes heavy with blame. It leads the blackbirds along the riverbank in a cry.

I yell Okalee's name.

I watch the riverbank for any sign of movement, for a bright yellow form slumped in the mud.

She was in the middle of the river, the blackbirds say. *You would have seen her if she got out.*

And the reality and the knowing nearly push me to

my knees, and I stagger, but I can't kneel because if I do I will have to accept this and I won't. The river's roar sounds dull in my ears. I try to scream her name again but the blackbirds beat me to it, snapping the silence.

O-ka-lee! O-ka-lee!

I don't realize my eyes have shut on me until I hear footsteps pounding over my head and Wardie's voice shooting through the bridge slats. I'm slumped against the concrete pilings under the bridge, knee-deep in water.

"Hey! What are you doing down there?" *Pound pound pound.* "It's way too early to be in the river."

I force myself to open my eyes. To look at the world.

Clouds suffocate the sky. Nothing moves along the riverbank. The willows don't rustle, the aspens don't tremble, the spruces don't sway.

"Phoebe, it's really high today," Wardie says. "You should get out."

My mouth won't open to answer him. The water laps cold against my knees. The hairs there prickle and rise.

"Phoebe? Are you okay? Talk to me."

"I lost her." My voice cracks. "Okalee."

"Lost her? What are you talking about?" When I don't answer, he scrambles away. Moments later he sloshes through the water and stands next to me. He presses his finger into my shoulder. I watch my skin turn yellow-white and then shift back to gray-blue.

"Phoebe." Wardie taps me again. "What's going on? Where did you lose Okalee? Not in the river, right?"

"Yes, in the river. I lost her in the river." A desire fills my body and threatens to split my skin like an earthquake hammering at the seams of the earth: I want my sister to be in her room, kneeling on her desk chair with her tongue sticking out of the corner of her mouth as she draws a mountain scene or writes a poem.

Wardie grabs my shoulders and he's yelling. "Where is Okalee? Where did you last see her?"

I scrunch my eyes shut. "In the river."

My knees go hollow, and I drop into the river. The iciness of it tiptoes into my spine and climbs each knot of my backbone.

"What?" Wardie slides his hands under my armpits and lugs me back up. "Why was she in the river? I don't get it. That's crazy, Phoebe, seriously."

I shake my head. "We have to find her."

"Come on." Wardie grabs my arms and tugs me toward the bank, where I collapse into the mud.

"Phoebe." He shakes my shoulders again. "We gotta hurry. I know what you're supposed to do when stuff like this happens. I'm a ranger."

"You're not a ranger yet. What do you know?" I shove my hands into Wardie's chest. He staggers into the mud.

The blackbirds in the reeds call out to me.

O-ka-lee? Where is she? Phoebe, what have you done?

Ten minutes later I'm standing on the riverbank with Wardie, his mother, and two officers. One of them is Officer Mason, Wardie's father. The other introduces himself as the chief deputy coroner.

Coroner. What does that word mean? I've heard it before. I want to ask Okalee; she would know. But she's not here to tell me.

The answer comes to me anyway. *A person who deals with all the dead people in the county.*

My bones start to shake.

"Phoebe." Officer Mason lays a gentle hand on my shoulder. "We'll talk about what happened later. Right now, we need to start the search." His gaze is kind but professional. Efficient. Concerned. "Where did you last see her?"

What do I say?

Car doors open and slam shut, jarring me. More people join the group, tugging on wet suits and goggles. Search and rescue divers.

"Phoebe?" Officer Mason says again. "Where did she disappear?"

The scene replays in my mind again. The boulder. She

43

surfaced again a few feet downstream from the boulder and then she went under and I never saw her again.

I dig my heels into the pebbles and mud and try to think of anything but that moment. A little gray bird plods along the shore. An American dipper.

"Miss," the coroner says, "can you stand where you were standing when you last saw the victim?"

The victim? I stare at the mustache sagging over his lips.

"He means Okalee, sweetheart," Mrs. Mason says. She touches my trembling white hand with her warm brown fingers and squeezes, encouraging. "Where were you standing when you last saw Okalee?"

Step, step, step. I stop midway up the sloping bank.

"That's where you were standing?" The coroner writes something down.

"Yes. I couldn't find her in the house," I say slowly, "so I ran out here and that's when I saw her. In the middle of the river."

I close my eyes. *What are you doing?* My body trembles with the effort it takes to speak the lie. They can't know I let her go into the swollen river, that the whole stupid ceremony was my idea. The lie keeps growing in my head like a tumor. Panic rises in me like a river current.

If Mamá and Dad find out I let Okalee go into that swollen river, if they find out River Day was my idea, I'll never be plain, strong, bad-grades, good-singer Phoebe ever again. Instead I'll be the daughter who let their Okalee drown.

Could anyone love that kind of daughter?

Their voices echo in my head. Mamá, after I told her about my solo. *I'm proud, hija. We haven't heard that beautiful voice of yours sing from a stage for too long.*

Dad, this morning. *Take good care of your sister.*

If they knew the truth, they'd never say *I'm proud* again.

They would never trust me again.

"Miss." The coroner's voice jabs my brain. "Miss!" I make myself look at him. "Now I need you to point to the river. Show me where you last saw the victim."

I flinch. "Her name's Okalee."

"I'm sorry?" The coroner pauses in his writing and cups his hand to his ear.

"Okalee." I'm breathing hard, and I want to slow down but I can't. "That's her name."

"Okalee, then," he says, as though I've just named a puppy. This is just another day on the job for him, I realize, and suddenly I hate him.

"Where did you last see Okalee?" he says. Creamy saliva pools in the corner of his lips, stretching in strings as he talks. How many dead people has he looked at this week without cleaning his mouth, with that same bland stare?

I can't look at him. I point to a spot just downstream of the boulder. The exact spot where I last saw Okalee.

"Son," Officer Mason says to Wardie, who's been hanging back until now. "Come over here and stand with Phoebe." Sorrow laces his words.

Wardie walks slowly toward us, his head down. I stare at the top of his head, his dark-brown hair. I want him to look at me, to tell me that this'll be okay. That we'll find her.

But he shoves his hands in his pockets. He doesn't look at me.

"See that diver, Phoebe?" Officer Mason says.

I stare at the river, but I can hardly see. It's as though my eyes are full of campfire smoke, stinging and watering. I make out a swimmer in a wet suit with a web of black and yellow gear that makes her look like a water monster. She holds up her hand.

Officer Mason looks at me. "Is the swimmer in the right place? Is that where you last saw her?" He pauses, clears his throat. "Okalee?" His voice breaks over her name, a stick snapped over a knee.

I take a good hard stare at the swimmer and try not to cry. I motion her to the left. She shifts in the current and then shoots me a thumbs-up. My shaking thumb rises to match hers. Two more swimmers wade into the Grayling. The river sloshes around their boots.

Please find her.

"Phoebe?" Officer Mason says softly. Wardie stands next to him, hands still buried in the pockets of his pajama pants. "Now that we've got the search going, I need you to tell me exactly what happened."

I cannot tear my eyes away from the river. *Okalee, Okalee, what do I tell them?* But I already know that whatever I say, it won't be the truth.

Forgive me, sister.

Officer Mason takes a pen from his uniform pocket.

I open my mouth to speak the deepest lie of my life.

5

Before I can say a word, Mamá barges around the corner of the house. How'd she get here so fast? Someone must have called Mamá or Dad and told them what happened. She sprints down the slope to the river-bank, bright-red scarf flapping like it's chasing her.

"¿Adónde? ¿Adónde está?" Her voice is high and wild. She reaches Mrs. Mason and clutches her best friend's arm, swaying like an aspen tree in a strong wind. Mrs. Mason tries to steady her, and I'm halfway to her, but Dad beats me there, long legs carrying him swiftly to her side. He cradles her against his chest. He beams his gaze on the riverbank, a lighthouse looking for his lost daughter. His eyes pass right over me. I am not the one he wants.

"She's not here yet. They don't know yet, Soledad," he says. "They're going to search, all right, love?"

"Where are the dogs? Los perros? They need to bring

dogs to smell." Mamá tries to squirm out of Dad's arms, but he hangs on to her.

Officer Mason wipes his glasses and sets them, heavily, on his nose. "We're bringing search dogs right now, Soledad. While we wait, we need to talk to Phoebe about what happened."

I'm five steps away, and I can't move. Officer Mason exchanges a look with Dad, who seems to realize that I'm here, hurting just like them. He shuffles over to me and crouches so that he and I are eye to eye.

"Are you okay?" he says. "You're not hurt?"

"No," I whisper. No, I'm not okay. No, I *am* hurt. Can't he see it on my skin, on my fingernails? Can't he hear it in my voice?

"Can you tell us what happened?" He reaches out to touch my cheek.

I nod. Guilt pulses through me, hot and heavy and stinging. I burrow into Dad's arms, and he holds me tight.

"Okalee wanted to go in the river today," I mumble into his flannel shirt. That much is true. I take a shuddery breath. "She's been working hard at swimming lessons. She wanted to test her skills in the river. I said no way could she go in. I think . . ." I pause. Dad waits, his breathing heavy. "I think she kinda took that as a challenge."

That's true, in a way.

Officer Mason's pen scritches across his notepad. "I

understand your parents left you in charge of your sister. Did your sister tell you that she was going outside? Did she tell you what her plans were this morning?"

"I made her promise she wouldn't go in, after she told me. But she did anyway, while I was in the bathroom. I would never have let her go in the river on her own," I say. My tongue feels too big, too thick, yet the lie slips out so easily. "After I got out of the bathroom, I couldn't find her anywhere, and then I ran outside and she was all the way at the boulder. And then she just—"

I swallow and try to speak again, but the words reach my throat and shatter there.

"All right, Phoebe," Officer Mason says, laying his heavy hand on my shoulder. "Thank you. I know that was hard."

I hide my face in Dad's shirt. Mamá murmurs something into my ear. I want to draw comfort from them, but I can't. All I want to do is coil my arms around my sister's warm shoulders and never let her go. I want to bury my nose in the crook of her neck and smell the rosemary and juniper soap on her skin. I want to whisper into the soft curve of her ear that I love her, I love her so much.

"Dios ayúdanos," Mamá whispers finally. She squeezes my hand. Then her voice gets stronger, and she lets go of me. "Lars, we need to go. We need to search." She turns to me, eyes fierce. "Do not go near the river, Phoebe. Don't you dare touch the water."

"You'll be all right?" Dad asks me. I nod. He and Mamá and Officer Mason jog to the river, and for a moment, I stand alone. Then someone lifts a quilt over my shoulders. I turn and look straight into the sad, kind eyes of Ms. Loring.

"I hope it's okay that I'm here," she says. "I came as soon as I heard." She opens her arms, and I let myself fall into them.

More people arrive: Mr. Ripwinkle, striding purposefully toward Officer Mason and the coroner. Mrs. Dixon, Okalee's teacher. A woman I recognize as Mamá's boss, holding an armful of quilts and passing them out to search and rescue divers resting on the riverbank. A pair of women holding German shepherd dogs straining at the leashes. Wardie, coming out of my house with one of Okalee's shirts laid carefully over his two hands, like he's holding a platter bearing something precious. Okalee's best friend, Cora Henry, pacing the riverbank with her older brother. Kat Waters, who looks wary and pale, trailing behind her mom and dad.

And, walking slowly down the incline toward me, Helena.

I break away from Ms. Loring and lurch toward Helena.

She clutches me; we bury our faces in each others' shoulders.

"What happened?" she whispers.

"She went in the river, and we can't find her."

"All by herself?"

I nod, my cheek scraping her collarbone. An icy breeze spills down the back of my shirt. "I don't know why she did it," I say.

Helena's arms stiffen. But I'm not really talking about Okalee, I'm talking about me. Why would I let my own sister wade into the river alone?

She pats my back. "I don't know."

Before long I feel the presence of someone standing near, waiting to speak to me. Officer Mason stands before us, holding a pink hoodie with the word *adidas* printed in white over the chest. Dirt is streaked across the white, smudging parts of the letters brown.

"One of the searchers found this a ways upriver while he was knocking on doors." Officer Mason looks at me. "Is it Okalee's, by any chance?"

Helena lets go of me. "I'm gonna go see if my parents are here yet," she says.

I shake my head, relief rolling through me. It's not Okalee's hoodie, which means it's not some piece of her clothing that the river ripped off. Maybe the river didn't

knock her around too fiercely, and she's out there somewhere, whole and lost and searching for us.

"We've found no sign of her yet," Officer Mason says.
His shoulders slump, and he becomes Mr. Mason, kind
and soft and smelling of cinnamon and butter. "I'm sorry,
Phoebe. If you'll come with me, I need to have a word with
you and your parents."

Numb, I follow him to where Mamá is standing in the
river with Mrs. Mason, a quilt hanging loosely over their
shoulders.

"Lars went to search," Mamá tells Officer Mason. She
looks at me, her eyes so full of hurting that I have to look
away. Mrs. Mason squeezes her tight. Mamá leans her head
on Mrs. Mason's shoulder.

"We need to talk about what could have happened to
Okalee, Soledad. I wish Lars were here. We can wait for
him if you—"

"No. Dime." *Tell me*. Her head snaps back up. She's
hungry for every detail.

"When somebody inhales fresh water into their lungs,"
Officer Mason says, "it passes into the blood and dilutes
blood cells. In just a few minutes, the bursting cells cause
organ failure and . . ." He hesitates, lays his hand on
Mamá's shoulder. "And then death. Forgive me; I'm not
saying she's passed away, but—"

"You did not do anything wrong," Mamá says. "But I won't give up on my girl until we find her."

The coroner ambles up to us. He must have heard Officer Mason's last words because he says, "Miss Petersen pointed out to the searchers where she last saw her, but they haven't found a body there. The current is pretty strong, so we think in those two or three minutes she could have gone quite a ways downriver. Once the body dies, it sinks to the bottom of the river where the current is much slower. We hope to—"

"Espera." Mamá holds out her hand, stopping his words. "Until she is found dead, there is still a chance she is alive," she says firmly.

The coroner shakes his head. "That's wishful thinking. See—"

"Jerry," Officer Mason warns.

But the coroner continues, shrugging. "I mean, they've got the dogs sniffing the banks on both sides, but they're not picking up her scent there. I'm sorry to say that we're pretty sure she didn't make it out of the river."

He doesn't sound sorry enough, not for what has happened.

Mamá folds her arms across her chest and shakes her head.

"Soledad, the Civil Air Patrol is going to send a helicopter out as soon as the sky clears up," Officer Mason says.

"We're attacking this search from every angle. This river's a fast one, but we'll do our best to find her."

"She's got to come up some time," the coroner says. His eyes take on a sickly eagerness. "As her body decomposes, it will fill with gas, and she'll be lighter than water. The river's pretty cold, so it may take a week or two, but the body—"

It's too much. I drop to my knees in the gravel and wrap my arms around my head, my elbows clamped over my ears. I rock back and forth, back and forth. "Okalee Okalee Okalee," I moan, and I know I sound like a dying animal, but I don't care one bit.

"Stop talking, Jerry," I hear Officer Mason snap. "Dulce! Wardie!"

I smell Mamá's vanilla and black currant lotion right before I feel her hand on my back. "Jesucristo ayúdanos," she whispers brokenly.

Mrs. Mason kneels too, reaching for my hand. I grab it and hold it tight. "I'm here," she says. "I won't go."

Then more hands fall on me, and I hear Wardie's voice, higher than usual. "Hey, Phoebe, I'm here too, okay? I'm here."

He's crying. He wraps his hands around me, and it's awkward, all bony elbows and tears and snot, but it's what I need. I breathe him in, his fear and his wild scent of sap, of pine. He smells safe and good and truthful. Mamá's hand rubs my back in long, soft circles.

Wardie takes two shaky breaths and lets go of me. "I'm sorry I yelled at you," he says softly. "I know it wasn't your fault that Okalee went into the river. We all know that if she wants something, she'll do it no matter what anyone says."

So everyone knows my lie now. I can't answer him. I can't even nod. Thunder explodes in the clouds over Lone Peak.

The thunder knows the truth. The river knows. The grasses and the aspens and the willows know.

Rain starts plucking at the Grayling. I unfurl my body and watch the rain weep down my shivering knees.

↟ ↟ ↟ ↟

They find her later that night, three miles downriver, fingers tangled in a branch caught in the river. I'm not supposed to be there, but I can't stay away. I can't leave my sister again.

Dad and Officer Mason scoop her out of the water. Officer Mason's flashlight shines through her skin like it almost isn't there, like breath on a freezing winter morning.

Dad kneels on the mud. Mamá kneels too, her breath hitching, her lips quivering. She gently takes Okalee from Dad and rocks her back and forth, back and forth. Softly she sings a Cuban lullaby that Okalee and I used to beg for every night when we were little.

Duérmete mi niña, duérmete mi amor,
Duérmete pedazo de mi corazón.

Dad presses his lips to Okalee's forehead. "My precious Blackbird," he whispers. He folds his hand over her eyes, closing them against the rain.

Sleep, my love, piece of my heart.

I bend down to whisper, with an aching voice, *I'm sorry, sister; I love you so*, but the words don't come, and I know it's because I don't deserve to speak them.

6

Tuesday night, I stand on the stage in the darkened Grayling Crossing Community Church, staring at the pine box resting before me. The church is hushed, and all eyes solemnly watch me. This time the nerves are buried deep down inside where they can barely touch me. I feel like a piece of driftwood caught at the river's edge: stuck, lifeless, watching people rush on with their lives. Even these people at the funeral, they won't cry for Okalee forever like I will.

It's time to sing my sister, my blackbird, into the next part of her journey, as Mamá put it. But I don't know what that even means. Isn't she already gone?

For me, this song for Okalee will be my way of saying how sorry I am. I will sing my apology into this quiet, wood-smelling church, and it will be the most important thing I ever do.

Mamá sits on the steps next to the casket, cradling her guitar. She's wearing a simple black dress. No colorful scarves, no makeup. Her hair is in a limp ponytail. She seems like a shadow of the Mamá I know. Dad says she needs her time to grieve. She hasn't taken a real shower since River Day; she says the sound of water hitting the bathtub makes her sick. Dad has to remind her to drink water at least three times a day, and even then she barely gets it down.

Water, the river—it terrifies her. Dad even has to make her Cuban coffee for her.

I want the old, vibrant Mamá to come back. Then I feel guilty for even thinking that.

Earlier Mamá wept silently as she laid her most prized quilt, the one with daisies and lilacs and wild roses printed all over it, over top of Okalee's casket. I can't see Mamá's expression from here, but I know it's either tugged down in sadness or blank and exhausted, like she can't see anything around her, like none of it matters.

I keep waiting for her to grab me by the shoulders and ask me what really happened the day Okalee drowned, but she hasn't yet, and then I remind myself that she doesn't know I lied. She got angry with the *Bozeman Daily News* last night because—not two days after Okalee drowned— they ran an article about Okalee. In it, they printed the exact words of my lie, and they also printed coroner Jerry's opinion of my sister: *It was a very unwise decision. You would hope the girl had a healthy respect of the river, seeing how that portion of the Grayling runs through her backyard.*

I know each of the families in here has read it. The Ripwinkles, Ms. Loring, the Masons and McClains, Cora Henry and her family, Kat Waters and her parents— they've all read it. Everyone in the Gallatin Valley thinks Okalee made a decision no Montana girl should ever be dumb enough to make. Ten-year-old kids shouldn't drown, they said in the comments. They're too smart to wade into rivers. It's the little ones who'll wander in on accident.

These people watch me now, expectant.

Yesterday, Mamá asked Dad which song Okalee would like best, and I suggested her favorite: "Auld Lang Syne." To me, it's a sad song, but Okalee loved that about it. She said it was "deliciously sad." Mournful. She and Mamá and I made our own version of it using the guitar, and even though Okalee's voice sounded like a screech owl, we would sing it all year, not just on New Year's Eve.

Tonight, just Mamá and I are singing it. I'm starting out alone, but she will join me with her plain, steady soprano harmony partway through.

I think about the words I'm preparing to sing.

> *Should old acquaintance be forgot,*
> *and never brought to mind?*

> *Should old acquaintance be forgot,*
> *and auld lang syne?*

I breathe heavily. The microphone resting on a stand in front of me catches all my sounds and scatters them into the chapel. Mamá begins to strum her guitar. She looks at me, her lip already trembling. This is where I'm supposed to come in.

I open my mouth to sing the words. "Should old acquaintance be forgot," I whisper, but it doesn't come out as singing. It's a spoken phrase, and it sounds like a plea. Worry creases Mamá's forehead.

My skin pricks hot under my scratchy dress. The onlookers in the pews clear their throats.

Mamá strums on, nodding at me as if to say, *You can do this*.

But now I have to wait until the next verse to come in smoothly. *Get it together, Phoebe*, I think firmly.

I concentrate on the words I need to sing next.

> *We two have run about the slopes,*
> *and picked the daisies fine;*
> *But we've wandered many a weary foot,*
> *since auld lang syne.*

As I think them, the words stitch through my heart and pierce it over and over. Because all I can think about is picking flowers with Okalee last spring. Rolling my eyes at her every day when she sat at the table, a pile of home-work in front of her. Holding her hand when we crossed the river. All I can think of with this song about saying goodbye to the old times is that those memories are all old times now, for real and forever. And every single memory is polluted by the lie I told.

I gather my voice in my throat and prepare to try again. I've got to sing for my sister. After everything I've done, it is the very least I can do for her.

But I've missed the cue. Mamá's frustration radiates off her back. Sweat slicks the skin of my neck. I decide to just jump right in and not wait for the last verse, the one where I'm supposed to harmonize with Mamá.

But only a croaky whisper leaks from my lips. My throat feels tight and heavy and aching.

I shake my head. What is wrong with my voice?

The congregation shuffles, uncomfortable. Mr. Mason holds his head in his hands. Wardie is riveted by some-thing in the program. Helena sits between her parents, tears dripping off her downturned chin.

Only Dad and Cora Henry are still looking at me. Dad's eyes are full of pity. Cora's slide away. A lock of dark-brown hair falls over her eye, and she doesn't move it away. Her chin quivers. It's like she can't believe what is happening—can't believe that I'm failing to sing for Okalee.

I shake my head again. I want to shrink into myself

and evaporate into the dark, candlelit air. "I'm sorry," I say softly. The microphone amplifies the fragile words into the chapel, making me cringe. And then, as Mamá strums on by herself, I kneel next to Okalee's simple casket with the only shred of dignity I have left and rest my cheek on its quilt-draped lid.

Mamá's strumming grows forceful. *Why aren't you singing, hija?* I can almost hear her say. *Look how I am playing for my daughter. But you have let her down.*

"I know," I murmur into the fabric. It smells like our house, like black beans and garlicky mojo, like dryer sheets, like Okalee's laughter.

Our house will never smell like that again.

Mamá starts to sing what is supposed to be our harmony, and the heat in my face burns all the good smells out of the quilt. I just want this song to end. And then I never want to hear it again.

> *For auld lang syne, my dear,*
> *for auld lang syne,*

Her words are thick with a Cuban accent and sadder than the song of a mourning dove.

> *we'll take a cup of kindness yet,*
> *for auld lang syne.*

The candlelight glints off the tears tracking down

Mamá's face, but she keeps singing, her voice growing as thin as a piece of fabric.

For auld lang syne.

The guitar lets out a last, sorrowful note, and Mamá rises, walks to Okalee's coffin, and kisses the wood resting over Okalee's face. "Te quiero mucho. Te quiero tanto. Te quiero siempre," she whispers.

I love you lots. I love you tons. I love you always. The nighttime blessing Okalee and I have received each bedtime of our lives.

I wait for Mamá to touch my shoulder and whisper the same thing to me too.

But she turns without looking at me and sits back down in the pew.

At the end of the ceremony, I stand next to Dad. Members of our community line up in the aisle to lay a daisy or rose on Okalee's coffin, and then they try to offer comfort, but none of it can fill the empty space beside us where Okalee should be standing.

"You sang beautifully, Soli," Mrs. Mason says, kissing Mamá's cheek. "I'm here for you, hermana. I'll bring you food tonight and stay if you want." Mamá nods and squeezes Mrs. Mason's hand.

Mrs. Mason looks at me, sympathy glimmering in her eyes. "Oh, hija" is all she says. She hugs me, and I wrap my arms around her to be polite.

I don't deserve her sympathy.

I failed to sing my apology to Okalee.

Wardie shuffles over, his hands jammed in his pockets. "Are you okay?" he says. He shakes his head. "I mean I know you're not, but, um, after the song thing . . ."

Is he thinking of my solo? About how just a couple days ago, I sang like an angel? About how now, I'm broken?

He rests his hand on my shoulder, squeezes lightly. The touch burns me, and it's like Wardie can sense that. He pulls away almost as quickly as he laid his hand down.

Good. I don't deserve the sympathy.

Helena's father holds his ten-gallon hat across his chest with one hand and rumbles an apology for what happened. He keeps his other big hand on Helena's shoulder.

She looks at me, her kind face pale and somehow thinner than it was last week. She opens her mouth and lifts her eyebrows as if to ask a question and then seems to snap out of it. She takes my hand in hers instead. "I don't know what to say."

"I don't either," I say. "Obviously. I can't even sing." I try to make it a joke, but any shards of laughter die somewhere in my chest before they can rise.

Helena shakes her head. What's she going to say—*it doesn't matter?* Because we both know it does. We both know how much it would have meant to Okalee to have me sing at her funeral.

"I'm sorry, Phoebe," Helena says helplessly. She hugs me too, her horsey hay-smell laced with sorrow.

Then Kat Waters appears in front of me. Her bob quivers at her chin. "I'm sorry for your loss," she says. She lays her thin hand on my wrist and says in a dramatic whisper, "Your grief has consumed your voice." She shakes her head. "You're in my thoughts. If you need me to sing the solo for you, I'd be happy to help out." She pats my wrist.

Her words probably sound innocent to the adults around us, but I know the truth. "Get away from me," I whisper. I jerk away from her touch, and she disappears into the crowd of mourners.

Cora Henry and her little sister, Gracie, come next. Cora glances at the crowd that had swallowed Kat. "Okalee would've told Kat off if she heard her say that." She points at her shirt. It's dark blue like the river in late evening. Printed in graceful, light-blue letters are the words "When you feel afraid, remember; Where one tree falls, more can grow."

In smaller letters below that, it says "Georgeline Morsette."

"It's from my and Okalee's favorite poem, 'Remember,'"

Cora says quietly. "By Georgeline Morsette, our favorite poet. She's Chippewa Cree, like me. Remember that poetry reading Okalee and I went to at MSU in December? She read this poem, and we both fell in love with it right away. We saved up the money to design and order these shirts, and they got here the day before—" She stops and swallows and takes something out of her bag. It's a folded, dark-blue T-shirt. She hands it to me. It's the twin of the shirt she has on. "This one was supposed to be for Okalee. But since she's not here, I want you to have it. It might fit you. It's a medium."

I can't speak. I hug the shirt to me. It's a gift from Cora, but it feels like a gift from Okalee too. "Thank you. So much." Cora nods, smiles sadly, and walks away with Gracie.

I open the shirt, ignoring whoever's next in line. A folded piece of paper falls out. I open it. There, in Okalee's perfect handwriting, is the full poem, written out. A note above it says, "My favorite poem of all time. I got to see the famous poet herself read it in person, and I fell in love. Goal: to memorize entire poem."

I can barely breathe. I touch the letters, and in some way, I can feel her there, behind them. I can feel the pencil and the hand that held it. Her hand.

Remember
By Georgeline Morsette

When you feel afraid, remember;
Where one tree falls, more can grow.
Even though sometimes it's hard to let go
Everything pushes and pulls for a reason.
Everything changes, just like the seasons.

When you feel incapable, remember;
The beaver does not build its dam in one night.
Even if what you do is not always right,
Every raindrop can be a river.
(The earth carries all the answers within her.)

When you feel unworthy, remember;
Every constellation way out in space
Means just as much as every freckle on your face.
So smile often, and cry even more
Because every river needs a good downpour.

The poem wraps around me like a warm, strong hug. I think back to Christmastime, when Okalee and Cora came back from a night of poetry readings so starry-eyed you'd think they'd met a movie star. They'd gone straight to Okalee's room to write poems.

I understand their excitement, now. There is something about this poem that makes me dizzy with courage. *When you feel afraid, remember; Where one tree falls, more can grow.*

Without looking at who's in line to hug me next, I dash away.

"Phoebe!" Mamá shouts, startling the mourners waiting to hug her.

"Let her be, Soli," Dad says.

"Kat," I shout, ignoring the stares that follow me out the front door of the church. The cold March evening raises goose bumps on my arms. Kat turns, surprised.

"Kat," I say again, breathing hard. The shirt feels soft yet somehow heavy in my arms, and I know—I *know*—that if I can just sing the solo on Saturday night, Okalee will forgive me for letting her go in the river. "I don't know what happened to me tonight, but I *will* be able to sing that solo."

A glint of anger flashes in Kat's eyes and then dies—or hides somewhere deep in her head where I can't see it. She purses her lips. "Go sleep for a week, Phoebe. You look pretty terrible."

She turns toward her waiting parents, her ballet flats crunching on the gravel parking lot.

"I'm not kidding," I call out after her. "I won't let anything stop me."

She waves at me over her shoulder as if to flick a mosquito off her skin and then scrambles into her family's car.

I have to find my singing voice, and I have to find it fast.

I need to sing for my sister one last time.

Helena's family drives past in their truck. Helena's forehead is pressed to the window, and I wave to her.

She looks right through me. And she doesn't wave back.

7

The minute we get home, Mamá sets her coat carefully on the table, takes a deep breath, and looks me full in the face. Her eyes are filled with a pain so intense I want to look away. Her mouth is a straight, frustrated line. But the thing that shakes me the most is the hollowness in the curves and lines of her face, the sense that something is missing from Mamá that's never gone missing before.

"¿Qué pasó?" she says. "Why didn't you sing?"

I drop my gaze. "I couldn't."

"What do you mean, *couldn't*? Is your throat hurting you?"

"My throat is fine. I just . . ." I stare past Mamá at the counter laden with casseroles and cards and lilies. "My voice didn't work. My singing voice."

"Your voice didn't work." Mamá closes her eyes as if she's saying a prayer. Then she opens them again. "You know, if Okalee had been the one in your position, she would not have let anything stop her."

Everything inside me freezes. "Okalee couldn't even sing."

"Okalee could do anything she put her mind to," Mamá says. "Anything."

Rage stings my whole body.

"She wasn't perfect," I say.

"She was perfect enough for me." Mamá turns away. She takes a casserole and sets it in the fridge. And another, and another. Dad walks in from the mudroom, his eyes red. His cheeks, usually bright like Mormor Ida's always were, are paler than a swan's wing.

"It's all right, Phoebe," he says. "It was too soon, is all. I don't know how we could've expected you to sing so soon after everything."

Mamá stops what she's doing. "I sang," she says evenly.

Silence descends on the kitchen. The rooster clock tick, tick, ticks.

"Well, I'm not you," I say finally. "And I'm not Okalee." My voice sounds choked and babyish. I look around for Okalee, for sisterly support, for an exchanged look that says *Can you believe Mamá blames me for not singing?*

But then I remember.

She's gone. And it's my fault.

I wake in the middle of the night, heart pounding, sweat pouring from my skin. My quilt lies crumpled at my feet. My breath comes in shallow gasps. Flashes of a nightmare spear my mind: a hand pushing my head below the river and holding it there, water gushing into my mouth and clogging my lungs.

The face staring at me through the sheen of river water is Mamá's, blank and hollow.

I try to shake the darkness off my shoulders, but it clings to my whole body.

I grab my alarm clock: 2:14 a.m. I decide right then that I'm going back to school in the morning. I can't bear to stay home all day with Mamá's blank and hurting stare.

I crack my window open to the cold night air and slink back under the covers. They're still warm, and I try to calm down and drift back to sleep. But even though the fragments of my nightmare have almost slipped away, I can't stop thinking about how, in five hours, I'll walk over the Oxtail Bridge without Okalee chattering at my side.

Wednesday morning, I slip between the school's glass double doors half an hour before classes begin. Ms. Loring sees me first.

"Phoebe!" She rushes over, enveloping me in a hug that smells like lilacs, like the springtime Okalee and I should be looking forward to right now.

I shove the pain down.

Ms. Loring pulls away. "You're back." She doesn't ask why I came so soon after Okalee's funeral or insist that I turn around and walk back home, and for that I am grateful. "I have someone for you to meet."

Before I can protest, she grabs my hand and leads me to the door of the old copy room. She knocks twice and almost immediately the door opens, and Dr. Santana, a tall Black woman with curly brown hair and warm, black eyes smiles at me. A mug of tea steams in her hand. I've seen Dr. Santana around the school since she replaced our old counselor a year ago, but I've never talked to her before.

"This is Phoebe," Ms. Loring says, her voice heavy with meaning. "Phoebe, I'm sure you've seen Doctor Eva Santana around. She is a wonderful counselor, and she'll be able to help you ease back into school life, all right, sweetheart?"

I nod. Dr. Santana reaches out to touch my shoulder, and instantly I like her. Maybe it's those eyes, or maybe it's that I suddenly realize the significance of her last name, Santana. She must be Latine, too.

"Phoebe." Dr. Santana smiles warmly. "Come in."

I sit in the first of two armchairs. On the small table

between the chairs is a flickering, lavender-scented candle, a Mason jar full of stones, a box of tissues, and a steaming mug of chamomile tea. It's almost as though Dr. Santana expected me to come. A lamp illuminates the room. Pictures of palm trees and old, colorful buildings line the walls. Blue, green, pink, yellow. I've never seen a cheerier-looking town.

"Puerto Rico," Dr. Santana says with a smile, taking a seat across from me. "My dad's from there." She points across the room to a photo of a white-sand beach, clear turquoise water stretching beyond it. "And my mom's Jamaican. She thinks I'm out of my mind for moving up here." She laughs softly.

Immediately I feel safe, cocooned away from the rest of the school. The pictures transport me to places I want to go one day with Wardie, Helena, and Okalee.

Jab. Not Okalee. Not anymore.

I look away from the photos and clear my throat. "So why did you move here?"

"My partner is from Montana. He convinced me to move here about five years ago now."

"You'll have to come to our tamale party," I say. "If we still have one this year."

Dr. Santana raises her eyebrows, so I explain. "My best friend Wardie's mom is from Mexico. I'm Cuban. On Easter, Wardie's mom throws this huge party where she and my mom make hundreds of tamales and anyone can come eat them."

"That sounds amazing."

I nod. Fellow Latine families definitely get special treatment at the tamale party because there's only a handful of us in Grayling Crossing.

Okalee loved the tamale party. She stuffed herself with pineapple tamales every single year. One time she threw up because she ate too many of them, but that didn't stop her from loving those tamales all the same.

"Yeah." My voice cracks, taking my mind right back to singing. Or not-singing, I should say. I tried to sing in the shower this morning, tried loosening my vocal chords with steam, but no song came out. Not one measly note. We have choir practice *today*. I have to sing the solo this afternoon, or else Kat might convince Ms. Loring to give it to her. Maybe Dr. Santana can help me get my singing voice back.

Dr. Santana folds her hands as if in prayer. Before she can speak, I take a huge breath and say, really, really fast before I lose my nerve, "MysisterdrownedonSaturday." The words bounce around in my skull. *My. Sister. Drowned. On. Saturday.* Ordinary words, on their own. A nightmare when you say them together.

Dr. Santana nods once, eyes kind under her fringe of curly bangs. "Yes," she says. "Tell me about your sister,

Phoebe. Her name is—" She glances at a piece of paper on her desk. "Okalee, yes?"

I grip the seat of the armchair, nodding. "She was perfect," I begin, and I can't keep the bitterness out of my voice. "Beautiful and kind and good at everything."

Her face surfaces—

The image swallows any other thoughts, and for a moment, it is all I see. My heart races. I press my fingertips to my temples. I take a deep breath. "She loved me. She loved to hear me sing—"

—she's four feet from me in the water—

I squeeze my eyes shut. Shake my head. "I can't do this."

Warm hands enfold mine. "Phoebe," Dr. Santana says in a low voice. "You can stay here as long as you like. If you want to talk about something that doesn't have to do with Okalee, that's fine too."

"I love to sing," I say to Dr. Santana. "Singing is . . ." I search for a way to describe it. "It's like breathing, for me. Before Okalee—" I can't make myself say *drowned*. But Dr. Santana nods as if she understands what I don't say. "I sang all the time," I continue. "In the shower, in the morning by myself in my room, while I walked along the river."

Dr. Santana folds her hands together and leans forward, as though it's the most important thing ever for her to hear every word of my story. I like her even more.

"But now," I continue, "I can't sing at all. I was supposed to sing for my sister's funeral, and . . ." The shame of that failure rises in me again. "I couldn't."

Now I lean forward. "This is a huge problem, Dr. Santana, because I'm supposed to sing the solo for the spring concert on the tenth. Okalee was in the front row when I auditioned, and she was so excited for me—"

One arm reaches for me, fingers clawed—

I close my eyes again.

"Take a deep, slow breath, Phoebe," Dr. Santana says.

I nod and suck air into my nose.

"Feel your rib cage expand. Feel the air sweeping into your lungs."

Okalee didn't get to breathe a good last breath, I think. *She had to breathe water.* Pain shoots into my lungs and crackles up my ribs.

"It hurts," I whimper. "Breathing like that really hurts."

Dr. Santana turns to her desk. "I'd like you to come visit me every day, Phoebe, for the rest of the school year. That means we could do this later, but you might be ready now." She presses something warm and smooth and round into my hand. A stone rolled perfect by a river.

"I want you to do something for Okalee," she says. "Do you think you can?"

She reaches for the Mason jar on the table beside me, and I take a closer look at it. It's full of rocks, yes, but the rocks have names written on them. *Lilly. Grandma B. Daddy. Baby Joel.*

"These are names of loved ones who have passed on," Dr. Santana says. "I'd like to invite you to add Okalee to the memory jar. You have the stone, and I have a marker."

The stone turns cold and hard in my hand. I look at Dr. Santana. "Memory jar?" What does that mean, that Okalee won't be a living person anymore after this?

But she's not living anymore, my brain reminds me. *She is a memory.*

No, not Okalee. I close my fist around the stone. I need to make Dr. Santana understand what I'm feeling.

"She was here on Friday," I say. "She sat in a chair in the auditorium. She swung on a swing at recess. She was *here.*"

I squeeze the stone harder.

"Hmm," Dr. Santana says. "What if I called the jar an honor jar? What if I said that putting Okalee's name on the rock would be a way to honor her?"

My hand slowly loosens on the rock. "Okay."

Dr. Santana hands me a Sharpie. I take my time writing Okalee's name down as perfectly as I can in small letters.

Okalee Luz

It doesn't seem complete.

"Can I write more?"

Dr. Santana nods. "It's your honor stone for Okalee."

So I flip the stone over and write *My Blackbird.*

There. Now Okalee lives on, on this rock.

I let the rock fall into the jar.

"How are you feeling, Phoebe?" Dr. Santana asks.

I almost say *guilty*, but I catch myself. "Okay, I guess." I take a breath. That's not a feeling. "I feel a little . . . shocked. Like, she can't really be in an honor jar, right? She should be sitting in her classroom right now."

Beyond the closed door I hear the bell ring, the laughter and squeaking shoes of kids rushing to their classrooms. Okalee would've been seated in her desk right now with her workbooks out and pencil poised over a notebook. No rushing for my sister. She's always—*was* always—overly prepared for things.

Dr. Santana leans back in her chair. "That's a normal thing to feel in a case like this. I don't tell many of my patients this, Phoebe, but I can see that you're having a great deal of difficulty right now, and I'd like to share something personal with you, if that's all right."

I nod.

"My first child, a daughter, died just a few days after she was born. She was born too early, you see. My body went into labor before it was ready." She leans forward again, settling her long forearms on her knees. "I blamed myself, my body, for failing my daughter. She was perfectly healthy, and if I could have kept her in me for just a week longer, she might've lived. But instead, she fought for two days, and then that was it."

"Did you hold her while she died?" I'm shocked at myself for asking this question. "I'm sorry," I say.

"I held her on my chest, skin to skin." Dr. Santana looks at me intently. "That's where she drew her last breath." Her shoulders drop just a tiny bit. "I didn't shower for a week. I didn't want to erase her from my skin. I still miss her and think about her every day, and that was seven years ago. She would've been just a couple years younger than Okalee."

I nod.

"A grief counselor had me draw that last moment with my daughter. It was the second-hardest thing I ever did, reliving that moment. At first I drew a rough sketch, but then I found myself adding more and more detail of my girl—her nose, the downy hair on her head and face. It was the beginning of my grieving process, that drawing. I framed it and have tucked it away in a place only I know about. From time to time, I take it out and look at it, and now I have positive memories as well as the painful ones."

"I can't draw," I say. "Drawing was Okalee's thing."

"Nevertheless." Dr. Santana hands me a fistful of markers and a clipboard with a blank page on it. "I'd like you to try to draw something. It doesn't have to be about that day. It can be a happy memory or a sad one or even one you don't understand. All I ask is that you draw something about your sister."

I take the clipboard, fingers dabbing sweat onto the clean page. I already know what I need to draw. Maybe if I draw it, it will stop haunting me.

I press the tip of the marker onto the paper. Almost as though it's possessed by another mind, my hand starts to draw, switching to a brown marker, then a peach one, a red one, a yellow one. Nothing in the world exists but this piece of paper, this childish scrawl of a drawing, and me.

I don't know how much time passes, but suddenly I'm done.

I stare at my paper. My skin prickles and goes hot. *Dr. Santana shouldn't see this.* I turn it over quick. *Unless . . .*

"Dr. Santana," I say slowly, "you have to keep secrets, right?"

"Unless you tell me you're going to hurt yourself or someone else, yes," Dr. Santana says. She takes a sip of her tea. Mine has gone cold in its cup.

I turn the paper back over and hold it out for her to see.

The scene is a river so brown it's almost black. One of Okalee's hands rests on the boulder; she's looking over her shoulder, back toward the riverbank. A red-winged black-bird looms over the rest of the page, its wings inky, and then, near its shoulders, blood red. Its beak is open and it's singing, but the gleam in its eyes is mocking me.

You're a liar, it says. *Liar, liar, pants on fire.*

At the edge of the river, so small you almost can't see it, stands a tiny stick person. The stick person has no muscles lining her arms, no strength. She's no match for the river, and she's waving at Okalee with both hands.

She's me.

I don't know if Dr. Santana can tell it's there, and I'm not sure if I want her to or not.

"Take a deep breath, Phoebe."

I make myself look at Dr. Santana, study her expression. She's concentrating on the paper. She definitely sees the stick person.

"Phoebe," she says, "is there anything you'd like to tell me?"

No no no no no. I think of Mamá's frustration, Wardie's trust, the kind look in Officer Mason's eyes.

Okalee.

Even if Dr. Santana can't tell anyone what I drew, I'm not ready for her to hear the most rotten thing about me.

I shake my head, crumple the paper, and shove it in my pocket. "I have to go to class."

8

The halls are blessedly empty. I stop at the bathroom and flush the drawing down the toilet, watching it swirl swirl swirl and—*whoosh!*—get sucked into the sewer.

Maybe Dr. Santana will forget about it.

Okalee's fourth-grade classroom is on the way to mine. Without thinking, I glance in the window. I stop short.

Classmates have covered every inch of her desk in flowers and pictures. But the space has never looked more bare to me, because Okalee isn't sitting there right now, and she never will again. The roses and sunflowers and framed photos are my reminders of what I've done. A hot, heavy knot of tears rises in my throat. I blink and blink and look away from the desk.

Slowly, I walk to my locker. Cards are taped all over its door too. *Condolences on Your Loss*, says one. *Praying for You*, says another. *In This Time of Grief* begins yet another.

More reminders. I open the door.

I've missed science class, but English is next. I take out the book we've been reading, *Little Women*. It's a book about sisters, one that Dad read to us when we were little. I always listened more to the soft rhythms of Dad's voice, but Okalee loved every bit of the story. She made me play-act the story with her at least once a week until she turned ten. She was always Jo, while I got to be whoever else was in the scene we were reenacting.

The thought of reading *Little Women* makes me feel emptier than this hallway.

The bell rings, and I jump and drop the book. Students pour out of classrooms. Lockers open and bang shut all around me, making me flinch. Chatter swells. Someone laughs loudly.

It's too much, this noise and clatter. I duck down to grab my book, and that's when I notice a folded piece of paper tucked into the pages like a bookmark.

I don't use bookmarks. I'm one of those people librarians hate who dog-ear books. I take the paper out. It's a note, printed from a computer.

WHY DID YOU LIE ABOUT THE WAY YOUR SISTER DIED?

My breath evaporates in my lungs. The words pop out of the paper, stark and accusing.

"Hey." Wardie sounds surprised, pleased even, to see me. I close my hand around the note.

"Hey." I try to make my face look normal. Inside, all I feel is panic.

"You're here," he says. Then he laughs, his face turning red. "Duh."

"Wardie," I say, "did you see anyone around my locker this morning?"

He shakes his head. "No, why?"

I shrug. "Just wondering who left all these cards and things." Another lie. How many will I have to tell before . . . before what? I just want people to mourn Okalee and leave it at that. No more news articles. No more notes.

Wardie nods and opens his own locker door. I shove my backpack into my locker. The half-closed zipper reveals a sliver of pink fabric.

The adidas hoodie. It was hanging in the mudroom next to our coats this morning, all innocent like it belonged there, and I grabbed it and stuffed it in my backpack as I left for school. I didn't want to see it in the house, another reminder of the worst day of my life. The school has a dumpster, and I'd planned to toss it in there where Mamá or Dad could never see it again, either.

Now, I think about what Officer Mason said when he showed it to me. *One of the searchers found this a ways upriver while he was knocking on doors.*

I remember seeing movement in the trees upriver just before Okalee plunged into the water. Could the movement have been a person who saw what happened to Okalee? And could that person have been wearing this adidas hoodie?

The panic turns into fear. Did that someone write this note? With a whoosh of terror, I realize that Kat lives upriver.

What Kat said last night at the funeral rushes back to me. *If you need me to sing the solo for you, I'd be happy to help out.* Did Kat see us at the river? Is she holding on to what she saw, to the truth she knows, in order to force me to give her the solo? If Kat wrote this note, if she owns this hoodie and she saw us that day, then I have to know. But there's only one way I can think of to find out.

I unzip the backpack, fingers trembling. Wardie and my other classmates filter back into their classrooms. I wait until I'm alone in the hallway again before I take the hoodie out. It feels stiff and scratchy and smells like all the bad things that happened on River Day. Like pine needles, the river. Like blame. I swallow hard and pull it over my head anyway. I dust off the mud streaks as best I can and straighten it over my torso.

Then, breath coming fast, I step into my classroom.

All chatter stops. Mr. Ripwinkle looks up. Some eyes look at me with compassion. Others look away. I feel like a deer in open season wearing this stupid hoodie, but I've got to concentrate.

Kat stares at me, her face paler than usual, her blond bob shaking at her chin. Her gaze flicks down to the hoodie and then back at my face before darting away.

Mr. Ripwinkle clears his throat. "Welcome back, Phoebe. Please, take a seat." He nods at the book in my hands as if to say, *Your sister may be gone, but I have a class to teach. Get on with it.*

I shuffle to my desk, throwing him a glare over my shoulder. Helena sits two desks away from me. She smiles weakly at me, and then the smile vanishes and she presses her hand to her temple. Last year when Wardie broke his ankle playing soccer, Helena held his crutches and helped him ease into his desk every single morning. But she doesn't even get up to hug me.

All at once, the hoodie feels so scratchy and rough and hot that I yank it over my head. A few people throw weird looks my way, but Helena doesn't look up from *Little Women*.

I shove the hoodie under my desk.

"Why are you wearing that?" Wardie whispers. "What are you doing?"

"It's nothing," I say. Kat peeks over her shoulder, giving the hoodie a strange look before turning back around. I notice she's wearing pink leggings.

Kat wears a lot of pink.

Mr. Ripwinkle starts reading from *Little Women*. I go stiff when I remember what part we were at on Friday. Beth is sick, and the sisters are all alone at home because their father got sick on the battlefield and Marmee is in a faraway hospital tending to him. Okalee made me play the dying Beth so many times. She played Jo, always healthy and fluttering around, spooning maple syrup into my mouth as medicine.

I close the book and rest my head in my hands. Mr. Ripwinkle reads, with an uncomfortable clearing of his throat, "Beth . . . called imploringly for her mother. Then Jo grew frightened, Meg begged to be allowed to write the truth, and even Hannah said she 'would think of it, though there was no danger *yet*.'"

The truth. I know what comes next. Okalee and Wardie and I played out this scene over and over again: the girls find out that Laurie telegrammed their mother with the truth, and she's on her way home to take care of her dangerously ill daughter. The sisters' relief is huge. In our play version, they always collapsed into each others' arms—and Laurie's—because the burden was no longer theirs to carry alone. Once, Okalee even made herself cry with the relief of the moment. Wardie and I were amazed.

I wish I could have that relief. I wish my lie could be

resolved as easily as that. I wish my lie didn't make me the worst person in the universe.

I wish the truth would make my mother come running to me with her arms flung wide. I think of how frustrated Mamá was that I couldn't sing for Okalee last night. How much angrier would she be if she knew I led Okalee to the river myself?

When the bell rings for lunch, I dart out of the classroom faster than anyone else and sneak into the darkened library.

I watch out the small window in the library door for Kat to walk by. A minute later, she appears, walking with Lucia and a guy from the eighth grade named Cohen. Cohen scares me; he's big and pale and burly. If I'm honest with myself, Kat scares me a little too, especially without Okalee here to help me feel confident about a situation like this. But I step into the hallway anyway.

"Kat," I say, "can I talk to you?"

Kat stops short. Cohen's buried in his cell phone and doesn't notice me. Lucia whispers to Kat, "Do you want me to come with you?"

Kat straightens her shoulders. "Go on to lunch," she says. She slips into the library with me. For several seconds, we stand face-to-face in the hushed space, hundreds of book spines watching us.

"You're back to school way too soon." Kat crosses her arms. "If someone in my family died, I wouldn't want to go back to school for weeks."

A knife twists in my belly. What is she saying—that I don't really miss my sister?

But then, I think Kat doesn't understand what it's like at home. She doesn't understand what it's like to have a mom who makes you feel like you'll never be good enough.

I narrow my eyes at her. "Maybe," I say. "But I wanted to be here for choir, so I can practice *my* solo."

"So you can sing now?" Kat asks. "It sure sounded like you couldn't last night."

I ignore her jab and draw the note out of my pocket, willing my voice to sound brave and strong. Inside, I'm an aspen leaf shaking in the lightest breeze. "Did you write this and stick it in my locker this morning?"

Kat leans closer and peers at the note. She moves her lips as she reads. Then she looks at me, genuine confusion on her face. "I didn't write that. Is it *true?*" Kat's eyes bulge. "You *lied?*"

Oh, no. Why did I show it to her? I should've just asked her if the pink hoodie was hers.

"No!" How many lies is that now? I run my fingers through my hair, and they snag on my tangle of waves. "It's not true. It's a mean joke, and that's why I thought maybe you did it."

Kat snatches the note out of my fingers and reads it again. "This doesn't look like a joke to me." She waggles it in front of me. "It looks like a question."

"You would know," I snap. "You wrote it."

"I really didn't."

I reach for the note, but she holds it out of my reach. She backs toward the door, then pauses. "Phoebe," she says slowly, "no one gets why your sister would even want to touch the river at this time of year. Everyone thinks she's kind of an idiot for taking that swim."

The smells in the library get sharper: musty books, the wet-dog scent of recently washed carpet. My heartbeat rings in my ears.

"Who is everyone?"

"It doesn't matter. It's just . . . if there's some other truth out there, maybe it should be told."

She tucks the note in the back pocket of her leggings. *What kind of leggings have back pockets?* I think numbly as she slips out the door.

"Kat," I call out. "The note is mine. Give it to me!"

She ducks back in. "I think I'll keep it for now, Phoebe. And maybe you shouldn't sing the solo today. Or at all, really." She vanishes into the bright light of the hallway.

I hang back. I want the library's darkness to swallow me.

I understand what she's saying.

If you sing the solo, I'll tell everyone about the note.

9

By the time the whole school files into the gym for choir practice at the end of the day, I feel frazzled. I walk slowly to the row of chairs in front. I stop before the chair Okalee sat in on Friday, staring at it as if maybe if I look long and hard enough, she'll reappear there.

"Phoebe?" Wardie touches my elbow. "Are you gonna be able to sing?" He glances at the chair. Silence hangs in the air for a moment. Then, "I can't believe she's gone."

"Me either," I say quietly. Kat walks past, gives me a look that says, *Remember what I said?* and pats her bag slung over her shoulder. I bet she's got the note in there.

"Wardie," I say, "don't let anyone sit in that chair."

He nods. I love him for understanding why. I can't stand to see anyone sitting in Okalee's chair. Not now. Not ever. I give Wardie a half smile and then find Ms. Loring.

She's breathless and red-cheeked, like she's excited about something.

"Ms. Loring? Can I talk to you for a minute?" I can't sing the solo until I get that note back from Kat.

She waves for the fourth-graders to sit quietly and then turns to me. "I want to talk to you too. I'm thinking that since the concert is so soon after Okalee's passing, it would only be right to honor her during the program. So I was thinking, for 'Down in the River to Pray,' since it's the first song, we could enter the stage in the concert hall at the Inn in the darkness with candles lit for Okalee. You'd walk in front, your song leading all of us. Then we'd form Okalee's name with the candles on the stage and let them burn while we finished singing. You could say a few words afterward, and we could pick one or two students who were close to her to speak as well."

I'm rooted to the sticky floor. My first thought is *no*. I don't have my singing voice yet. But then something clicks into place inside me. If I can honor Okalee in front of everyone like Ms. Loring wants, that will make up for my failure at the funeral *and* take away the awfulness of my lie. Okalee would forgive it all.

And I know if I can feel that forgiveness from her, I won't ever have to tell a soul the truth about what happened on River Day. People will eventually forget the terrible way she died, and the stone of guilt lodged inside me will get smaller and lighter and easier to bear.

I think of the note, hidden in Kat's bag. Would she really tell?

"Phoebe?" Ms. Loring clutches her music folder to her chest. "Does that sound like a good idea, or . . ."

"It does." I rush on. "But you know, I had a hard time singing last night. I think I need to smooth out my voice at home. Can you give me a list of vocal exercises I can do?"

She brightens. "Of course! I'll hand you a folder full of them after class."

I sit in Okalee's chair. *I'm going to find my singing voice, Blackbird,* I tell her. *I promise.* I wait for her to whisper something back from wherever she is, but all I hear is silence.

But then, for the tiniest second, I can almost feel the warmth of her rising through the metal seat. Instead of comforting me, it makes me ache all over.

I close my eyes. Ms. Loring quiets everyone and tells the rest of the school what she told me. I busy myself with glancing around and gauging reactions. Cora Henry sits up straight, her face eager. I make a mental note to recommend her as one of the speakers who will honor Okalee. Lucia rolls her eyes. I glare at her, but she doesn't see me.

Then, suddenly, Wardie places a slip of paper in my lap. "They said to give this to you," he says. He looks worried, and he watches me open the note. In Kat's tidy handwriting, it says, *This doesn't change anything.*

I crumple the note in my fist. Rage pulses in my fingertips. Why can't she just leave me alone? Kat's giggle pounds in my ears. The words on the shirt Cora gave me yesterday come back to me.

When you feel afraid, remember;

Where one tree falls, more can grow.

With a deep breath, I smooth out the note. "Wardie, do you have a pencil?"

He shakes his head.

"What doesn't change what?" he says, craning toward the note.

I slap my hand over it and turn to Helena. Earlier, she said she had a headache, and I hope she got some Tylenol at the nurse's office.

"Helena?"

We lock eyes for a moment. A flash of hope darts across her face.

"Can I borrow a pencil?" I ask.

She sighs, then digs around in her backpack and silently hands me a pencil.

I take it and look up at her. "Hey, is everything okay?"

She sits down by me. "That's what I wanted to ask you." She nods at the note. "Is everything okay? Kat's not bugging you, is she?"

The truth scrambles to the tip of my tongue, and I want to let it out. I want to tell Helena everything. But she can't know what kind of person I really am.

I manage a smile. "She's not bothering me. It's fine."

Helena looks at me for a long time, and I have to turn away first. I feel like I've failed her, and I don't know why.

Before I can worry more about it, Kat laughs out loud at something Lucia said, and the snorty sound brings me back to the paper in front of me. Using my free hand as a writing surface, I scribble words on the bottom of the note.

Oh yes, it does.

I pass it back to Kat, watching out of the corner of my eye as she reads it. She smiles a little. That's unnerving. Then she tucks the note in her bag, and a dull ache spreads through my belly, almost like I'm suddenly coming down with the flu.

"I don't feel so good," I say, panic heightening my voice. I hug my belly. "I think I'm going to—"

I retch. Thankfully nothing comes out.

Helena's hand descends on my back. "Oh my goodness, Phoebe. Let me take you to the nurse." She helps me stand up. Ms. Loring nods at us as we leave, concern creasing her white forehead.

"Are you sure everything's okay, Helena?" I ask, breathing hard.

"What do you mean?"

But I dry heave again. The slice of toast I'd managed to shove down my throat this morning slaps at my stomach. I catch my breath and gasp, "Something seems different since . . . you know."

Another retch.

"Shh, shh, let's get you to the nurse." She drags me to the nurse's door. "Mrs. Cruz?"

Nurse Cruz ushers me inside. She sits me down in a chair and holds a bucket under my chin. I gag, and my hot breath fills the bucket and sits heavy around my face. I wish hard that I could go back in time to Friday, when life was tough because of school but essentially simple. Mamá was whistling and mixing up lemon cookies for us to bake together after school. Dad was tired from his job but happy. Helena was excited and rooting for me to audition for *America's Voice*.

And Okalee was alive.

Now everything's a mess, and the weight of it makes me gag again, and finally all the sickness pours out of me and into the bucket. Nurse Cruz rubs my back with each heave of my stomach.

I miss all of choir practice. Helena stays with me in the nurse's office, bringing me water and ginger candies and talking with Nurse Cruz so I can rest. When the last bell rings for school, we slip into the muddy world. Helena rides off on Bo, saying she needs to take him to a vet appointment.

I'd convinced Nurse Cruz to let me walk home instead of calling Mamá because I wanted to be alone.

Now as I walk the narrow trail through the field by myself, I realize Helena never answered my question.

I come home to the familiar smell of after-school baking.

A slender shoot of joy blooms inside me. Mamá is baking! Even though Okalee's gone, she's keeping our ritual going, the one just for us.

"Mamá?" I call through the mudroom. "Why'd you start baking without me?"

But then I step into the cold, gray kitchen, and the joy shrivels up. The baking smell gives way to something sharp and bitter. A blackened casserole sits on the counter, and Mamá bends over it, weeping, her shoulders shaking, fingers clutching the handles.

I rush to her and yank her away from the pan. Bright-red blisters line the pads of her fingers.

"Mamá!" I cry. I shove her fingers under the faucet and turn on the cold water.

"No!" she yells, trying to pull her hands away.

"You need the water. Por favor, please, please." I hold

her hands tight. I'm stronger than she is, so I try not to squeeze too hard. I know she hates the water, hates the rushing sound the faucet makes. Like a river.

Finally, she holds still. Water pours over her burns. She shakes and sobs. I try not to fall apart too. "What happened, Mamá?"

"Lo quemé," she says, weeping. "I burned it, the chicken casserole."

"Está bien, Mamá. It's okay. The casserole doesn't matter." Where's Dad? I don't know how to treat a burn like this. Why did my mother do something a child would know not to do? "Dad!" I yell. I want to yell at Mamá too. Tell her to please wake up, please come back, please be my mother again.

"Sí importa," Mamá says. She uses her arm to wipe her face. Her curls, tangled and greasy, stick to her cheeks. "It matters very much."

The bedroom door opens, and Dad walks down the hallway, hair rumpled. He sniffs the air. "What's going on? Soli, are you—Soli!" He runs to Mamá's side. "Soledad, your fingers. Phoebe, go get the gauze and two big bandages from the bathroom cupboard."

I run for the gauze and bandages and dash back quick. Dad nods for me to set them on the counter next to the sink. Mamá's sobs slow until she's breathing normally.

"I'm fine," she says. I shake my head.

"Did you use oven mitts when you took the casserole out of the oven?" Dad asks.

Mamá doesn't say anything, doesn't move. Then, voice ragged, she says, "I don't remember."

"You don't—" Dad stops. He closes his eyes. He bends down and kisses Mamá's hair. "It'll be okay. It looks like these are second-degree burns. We'll put some ointment on them and bandage the blisters, and you'll heal in a couple weeks."

Tick, tick.

"I'll never heal," Mamá says softly.

Dad says nothing. He and I both know Mamá's not talking about her burns.

"I have some good news that might help us feel better," I say. Hope rises in my chest. Maybe my solo and the tribute will help Mamá to grieve. Maybe seeing how much people loved Okalee will help her feel less alone. And no matter how terrified she is of water, she'll have to take care of herself—shower, brush her teeth—for Saturday night.

"Ms. Loring decided to make the concert on Saturday a tribute to honor Okalee. We're going to start with my solo, and we'll be holding candles, and a few of us are going to say some things about her—"

"No." Mamá's voice is quiet and low.

My breath leaves me.

She looks down at the angry blisters on her fingers.

"What?" I say. Maybe I heard her wrong.

"No," Mamá says again. "I don't want them to do that. I don't want you to sing." She turns, slowly. "Your sister died three days ago, Phoebe. We buried her last night. And you think it's okay to get up and sing on Saturday when you couldn't even make a sound at her funeral?"

I can't convince any words to come out of my mouth.

Mamá's dark eyes fill with pain and frustration and tears. "You aren't ready. *We* aren't ready. You will not be singing that solo."

"Soli—"

"No, Lars. You said so yourself, last night, that she is not ready to sing yet."

"But it's important to Phoebe to sing."

"Lars." Mamá's voice is tight. She closes her eyes and squeezes her fists together.

Dad takes a deep breath. He rubs his stubble. He looks at Mamá for a long time, standing there with her eyes closed like she's waiting for something crucial to happen and she can't look for fear it won't happen at all.

He blows a hard breath. "All right, Soledad. You're right." He doesn't sound too sure about it, though, and he lays his hand on my shoulder. "I'm really sorry, Phoebe. But Soli, I think we should let the school honor Okalee. Let them do that much at least."

Mamá nods, just barely. "Fine."

Dad squeezes my shoulder. "We need time, Phoebe. All of us. You too. You need time to grieve before you take on any big commitments."

I can't believe this. My throat feels tight and hot, but I force the words up through it. "Please. I have to sing. It's my way of honoring Okalee."

"I said no," Mamá says. "You had a chance to honor your sister last night." She steps close. "Prométame. Promise me you will give up that solo."

I back away from Mamá and Dad, but Mamá's arm snakes out, and she takes hold of me, the burns pulsing hot against my wrist. "Promise me. Por favor."

I carefully peel her fingers off my skin. "You should put your fingers back under the water," I say as calmly as I can.

Mamá shakes her head, like she's never been so disappointed in me in her life, and then she turns her back on me.

I stare at her dark curls, at the knobs of her spine pushing against her shirt. She's hardly eaten in three days, and it already shows. Soon every soft curve Okalee and I knew and loved will be gone.

"Phoebe—" Dad begins, but I run to Okalee's room and slam her door behind me.

I dive under my sister's covers and drink in her smell: the rosemary, the sweet almond, the soft scent of her skin.

It's still buried in her sheets, but I can tell it's fading. I clutch her quilt tight around me.

"Can you believe it, Okalee? They want me to drop out of the concert. Do you remember how excited you were on Friday when Ms. Loring announced that I won the solo?" I wait for her to answer. But I don't feel her presence anywhere.

"Don't worry, sis," I whisper. "I will sing for you on Saturday no matter what."

I promise.

Mamá's and Dad's voices rumble through the crack under the door. Mostly Dad's voice.

After a few minutes, the talking stops. Silence rings in my ears, and through it a long-buried memory swims into the murk of my mind. Preacher Ellison, who did Okalee's funeral, giving an Easter sermon about Judas Iscariot, who betrayed Jesus with a kiss. Preacher Ellison saying, "Can you imagine how Judas felt when Jesus looked at him as the soldiers led him to his death?"

Another memory burns up my spine, but I block it with all the mental force I have. *Push it down hard.* Part of it slips into my mind anyway: Okalee's arm reaching for me. And what came next: the water pouring into her mouth, the way the sun shone on her closed eyelids—

No. Remember what really happened?

It takes every ounce of my strength not to let the entire

truth of River Day claw its way into my memory. By the time the half-formed images spit me out, I'm a rotted mass, shaking and nauseated, with sweat trickling into my ears.

You did that to your sister, and everyone thinks she's a stupid kid who did it to herself.

I am worse than Judas. I betrayed Okalee, my blood, my sister.

And that's the reason I have to sing for her on Saturday night, no matter what Mamá and Dad say or do. It's the only way to let her know I'm sorry.

It's the only way to ease the weight of the guilt trapped inside my bones.

10

I'm the only member of the family to show up for supper. There's a reheated sympathy meat loaf on the table next to a sticky note covered in Dad's scrawling handwriting: *P, we went to visit your sister. Didn't want to bother you. Please try to eat. We love you.—Dad and Mamá.*

I sit at the table. The charred, lumpy casserole is still on the counter, which is piled with food and flowers and cards. There's also a picnic basket full of lemons, a stack of sunshine from Mrs. Mason.

Dad's note talks about Okalee as though she's somewhere they can sit and share a cup of hot chocolate with her and chat about life. But she's not. They're going to visit a patch of earth strewn with flowers and marked with a temporary wooden cross.

"It's crazy, isn't it?" I say, looking at the lemons. "It feels impossible. We really need your sunshine here, sister."

Pain shoots through my veins. It folds me in half, and with every beat of my heart, it *whoosh whoosh whooshes* through me, burning me, strangling my breath until it stops moving through my body at all.

The rooster clock on the kitchen wall ticks over and over and over before I can calm down. I breathe in a deep, slow breath like Dr. Santana said, trying to focus on the expanding rib cage, the air filling my lungs. I straighten in my seat.

Since no one's home, I tug the folder of voice exercises Ms. Loring gave me out of my backpack.

Following her instructions, I first drink a glass of water. Then I try to breathe deeply again, through my diaphragm, like she has us do in choir. But breathing like that still hurts; it feels like air from a negative-thirty-degree day is stabbing my lungs. So I breathe shallowly, because that's better than nothing.

Then I make a *brrrr* sound with my lips. *Brrrr, brrrr, brrrr.* Now time to move through my scales. *Do-re-mi-fa-so-la-ti-do*, all with this lip trill.

With as deep a breath as I can manage, I begin.

Brrrr, brrrr, brrrr, brrrr. I sit up straighter when I realize my voice is actually doing it. It's going up, down, up, down, hitting C4, D4, E4, F4. I breeze through the rest of the scales. I almost want to try to sing the solo right away, but Ms. Loring said to make sure my voice is thoroughly warmed up before I try, so I make myself move on down the list.

The next exercise requires a sipping straw, so I grab one from the kitchen. Then, blowing through the straw, I make a squealing sound from C4 to C5 and back down again. I do this three times, taking breaths before each set. Ms. Loring says this exercise helps decrease puffiness in the vocal chords.

Excited now, I move to the next exercise. *Make your voice like a silly cartoon, low in register, and say the word "gee" out loud, in a hee-haw manner.*

What on earth? I feel a smile break onto my face, the first real smile since River Day.

"Gee," I say, voice low. "Gee, gee, gee." I get sillier and dopier with each *gee*. I can feel the mechanisms in my throat being pushed down, made longer.

Now, like a whiny child or a braying donkey, say "Nay!" This will help you access your upper register.

"Nay!" I say, shrill and sassy. "Na-a-a-y!"

Then I'm done. I move through all the exercises one more time just to make sure I've squeezed all the usefulness out of them.

I close my eyes and imagine that I'm standing in the giant concert hall of the Grayling Crossing Inn. All the lights are off. I hold a candle with both hands, warm wax dripping onto my knuckles. The stained-glass windows, cathedral-high, glow in jeweled hues as the setting sun streams through them. My classmates stand behind me, holding their own candles. Everyone in the audience is watching, waiting. Hushed. I start to imagine Mamá and Dad sitting in the crowd but stop when I remember.

They don't want me to sing the solo anymore.

Don't think about that.

"As I went down in the river to pray," I say out loud— and that's what I'm doing, I'm saying, I'm speaking. My throat feels tight and achy and heavy, just like it did last night at Okalee's funeral. And just like at Okalee's funeral, I am not singing.

I grip the edge of the table and try again. "As I went down in the river to—"

Nope. My voice sounds flat, a first-grader reading a poem she hates without the slightest inflection.

"Come on, come on," I say. Maybe if I take a deeper breath, I'll be able to do it. I force my lungs to suck in as much air as possible. Pain ricochets through my chest and I cry out. "Come *on*!"

I stare at the rooster clock. *Tick. Tick.*

One more time. Maybe there's something to that third-time's-a-charm saying.

"As I went down in the river to pray, studying—" My voice crumples into a ball and shuts down on me.

I push away from the table and wipe the sweat off my

forehead. I pace back and forth across the kitchen floor. Then I stare at the black pieces of chicken in the burnt casserole. At the handles that burned Mamá's skin.

That's when I see the letters printed in neat permanent marker underneath one of the handles.

Brandi-Michelle Waters.

Ten minutes later, I'm hurrying across the bridge, cleaned casserole dish tucked under my arm. The lowering light glimmers on the river, begging me to look down and appreciate the beauty, but that river is not beautiful to me. Not anymore. I don't care if all the strength in my arms melts down to nothing. I'll never swim in it again.

Kat lives a mile and a half away. Wardie and I have walked past her house many times during our hikes into the foothills of the Moonlight Mountains. I'm on my way to give the casserole dish back to her mother, Brandi-Michelle.

And to do something else. Fear squeezes my heart when I think about what I need to do, but then I think of how if Okalee were alive, she'd be right here with me. We would've called this an adventure. A mission, even. The thought calms me down.

On Wardie's side of the Grayling, I stay hidden behind the spruces encircling his yard.

I hear an owl call, "Hoo-hoo. Hoo-hoo." I take deep breaths and tug my jacket tight around my shoulders. Then I start on the deer path that leads to Kat's house. Spruce and fir branches scratch my face with their thin, spiky fingers. A tussle in the brush to my right makes me stop cold, but then the bushes settle, and I know it's only the animals of the evening, busy with their hunting. Small animals, probably. Not bears or anything.

Please not a bear or mountain lion.

I remind myself that I know what to do if I meet one of those creatures: make myself big, loud, and brave if it's a black bear or mountain lion. Back away slowly if I see a grizzly, which I doubt I would, so close to Grayling Crossing. I remind myself that the forest is a second home to me, that the scary part of my evening isn't here between the spruces but in Kat Waters's house.

I start jogging. The casserole dish pushes against my ribs with each step. My breath spills from my mouth like plumes of smoke, and my skin tingles. I jog faster, leaping over exposed tree roots, dodging the arms of the evergreens. The river jabbers in my ear, but I push its voice away.

A ringing wail punctures the growing darkness. I stop to catch my breath. The single mournful note rises in pitch until it can't go on, and then it drops, a creek tumbling over a cliff. Water churning into a rocky pool. The howl rises again, and I tilt my head to the sky, listening. I know it's not a coyote; there's no wild laughter here, only a pure and lonely song that sounds like a warning.

What if it's telling me that what I'm about to do is too risky?

I almost turn around. But then the howl shudders into a bark and keens into the sky again, and somehow I know Okalee sent it. Somehow I know she really *is* here. Knowing she's with me gives me the strength to go on.

The wolf barks, gives a short howl, and then releases another long cry that wheels toward the cloud-cloaked moon.

About ten minutes later, I reach the Waters's residence, no wolf in sight. Here the trees are thinner, the Waters's one-story, L-shaped log house set farther back from the river than our house. I take a deep breath and walk to the front door. A cheerful wreath that says *Spring Is Here!* adorns it. I shiver and ring the doorbell.

Mrs. Waters opens the door. Like Kat, she wears her hair in a bob, but her hair is darker. She's thin and muscly and smiles sympathetically when she sees me. "Phoebe. What a nice surprise. Come in."

I ease into Kat's house. I've never been inside before. The kitchen is twice as big as ours and filled with shiny silver appliances. Kat and her father sit at a round kitchen table; Kat gapes at me.

"We were just eating supper," Mrs. Waters says. "You're welcome to join."

"It's okay," I say hurriedly. "I just came to bring your pan back." I hold out the casserole dish. "The casserole tasted delicious. I was wondering, since we liked it so much, if you could write the recipe down for me?"

I smile brightly at Mrs. Waters. I feel awful for this lie, but I need to buy some time.

"Oh! Of course." Mrs. Waters throws a look at Kat. "I told you that casserole would taste good, Katherine. It's a new recipe," she explains to me. "I'm not known for my cooking skills, and Kat likes me to stick to the tried-and-true."

Kat flashes me a smile. But I think she knows exactly why I'm here.

"Could I use the bathroom really quick?" I ask, pinching my legs together as though I've been holding it for an hour.

"It's the first door down the hall," Mrs. Waters says. "Kat, show her—"

"I can see it from here," I say, nodding at the open door in the hallway.

I slide past Kat and her dad, who's staring at his phone, and into the shadowy hallway. I wish the bathroom wasn't so close to the kitchen. I ease inside, feeling Kat's eyes on me the whole way, and turn the light on and shut the door. I take slow breaths to steady myself. After about a minute, I turn the doorknob as quietly as I can.

Nobody's in the hall. Kat's mother is talking to Kat, so Kat's back is turned to me. Perfect. I shut the door behind me, leaving the light on so it looks like I'm still inside the bathroom.

It only takes me a moment to find Kat's room because on the outside of the door hangs a pink letter *K*.

I slither inside. Her room is clean, much tidier than mine. A pink canopy hangs over her purple bed, and I reach out and touch it. I always wanted a canopy like that. A lamp sits on a white bedside table and shines golden light into the room. For some reason, I thought Kat's room would look meaner, like her. But instead it's pretty cozy.

Focus, Phoebe. I need to get what I came for and get out of Kat's room before she realizes I'm not in the bathroom anymore. I scan the bedroom for the black bag Kat had at school today. It's not on her desk or on any of her shelves, which are filled with singing contest trophies. I search her closet next, pawing past dresses and backpacks and a long, white nightgown like the ones Okalee and I wear at Christmastime when we celebrate St. Lucia's Day with hot chocolate and candles and the warm Lussekatter Dad bakes with our Mormor Ida's old family recipe.

Then, just when I hear footsteps start coming down the hall, I see the bag hanging on her bedpost, hidden partly by the foamy canopy. Part of me wants to hide. But I don't let myself, because I need the note. And I need to get it before Kat finds me. That's all that matters.

I dart to the bedpost and open the bag quick. I hold my breath and rifle through its inner pockets. My fingers detect a wallet, a tube of Chapstick, a sunglasses case, and then—*aha!*—I feel the folded square of my note.

Thump, thump.

I draw the note out. I unfold it to make sure it's the right—

The door bangs open. "Phoebe?"

I whirl around, note clutched in my palm.

"Get your fingers out of my bag!" Kat whispers. She checks over her shoulder and shuts the door. "What's in your hand?"

I stand up straight. "My note." I walk back around her bed and start to brush past her, but she puts her hand up.

"Wait." She shakes her head. "Do you think I'm stupid? Do you think I can't remember what the note says? I have it up here." She taps her blonde head.

"I don't care," I lie. "You don't have proof of anything if you don't have the note."

"But you think I wrote the note. Do you think I can't just write another one?"

"Aha!" I point at her. "You did write it!"

She looks amused. "Think whatever you want, Phoebe."

I drop my finger. "Whatever you think you saw, you didn't see what you thought you saw," I say, picking my words so carefully that what I say barely makes sense even to my ears. If Kat isn't the pink-hoodie girl, I don't want to give anything away.

Kat crosses her arms. "Wanna hear something interesting?"

I don't answer her.

"I did some poking around on my laptop earlier, and guess what I learned?"

I wait.

"Lying to the police is a crime." Her face turns serious. "I don't know how your sister really died. But someone does." She steps closer. "What really happened that day?"

I can't breathe. Kat takes another step.

"The story you told the police seems pretty shady. Your sister was smart enough not to go in the river alone. So what's the real story? Were you there with her? Did you do something to make your sister die?"

She's inches away from my face.

"Is that it? You lied because you"—she pauses, like she can't wait to slice me with the words she's about to say—"committed manslaughter?"

I blink and beg my face to stay straight and smooth, a river stone. "I told you," I say, trying to iron the trembles out of my voice, "whoever thinks they saw something that day didn't see what they think they saw."

Kat shrugs. "The truth always comes out. That's all I'm saying." She takes a step back. Opens her door. "You can hide all the notes in the world, and the truth will still come out."

I grab the recipe from Mrs. Waters, mutter a quick "Thanks," and practically sprint home. Dad is sitting on the couch watching some mindless reality show that he's never watched before. Mamá must be in bed. That's where she spends most of her time now. Dad sits up, worried, when I come in and starts to ask me where I've been, but I shoot past him and lock myself in the office at the end of the hall.

I log on to Google. My fingers quake. I know I committed crimes on Saturday. I knew it, deep in my mind, long before Kat told me.

But now I cannot wait one more second to find out what the consequences are for everything I've done.

Slowly I type, *Is it manslaughter if you accidentally cause someone's death?* I linger over that word—*accidentally*. I decide to include it because it was an accident. I never meant for Okalee to drown.

What I find chills me faster than a winter blizzard.

If the following three components have been met by the defendant, then he or she may be found guilty of involuntary manslaughter:

1. The defendant's actions caused someone's death.

My actions caused Okalee to drown. River Day was my idea. She wouldn't have been at the river if not for me.

2. The act was done recklessly, without care for human life, or was inherently dangerous.

By letting Okalee plunge into a dangerously high river, I showed carelessness with a human life. With my own sister's life.

3. The defendant knew or should have known his or her conduct was a threat to the lives of others.

I knew. I knew my conduct was dangerous. Isn't that the whole point of River Day—that we cross when it's a challenge? I almost canceled River Day when I found out Okalee wanted to cross alone, but I didn't, and I should have.

I take shallow, shuddery breaths and make myself search the next thing.

What happens when you lie to the police?

And what a surprise: that's a crime too. It's called false reporting. The very first description applies to me.

Montana Code Annotated 45-7-205. False reports to law enforcement authorities. (1) A person commits an offense under this section if the person knowingly:

(a) gives false information to any law enforcement officer with the purpose to implicate another.

That's exactly what I did. I gave false information. I implicated—I had to look that word up; it basically means *blamed*—Okalee for her own drowning.

The punishment for this offense is a $500 fine or six months of jail.

Or both.

I exit out of all the screens.

I have committed two crimes for which I could go to prison. I know I deserve it, but—

Oh, Okalee, tell me it's all right to go on with this lie. I can't survive jail. I know I can't. Losing you is hard enough already.

I pray that my sister will whisper something to me from wherever in this universe she's gone, or send another wolf to howl a message to me, or bring the song of a red-winged blackbird to the tree outside my window.

But I hear nothing.

11

On Thursday, I'm the first one in my classroom. When I settle into my desk at school, I find an envelope with my name printed on it.

Dread sweeps through me.

Helena walks into class, thick coppery braid slung over her shoulder.

"Helena," I whisper. "Did you see who left this on my desk?" I hold up the envelope.

Helena peers at it and then shakes her head. "I've been out with Bo. He's been acting weird after the shots he got yesterday. Maybe it's a sympathy card from someone?" She opens *Little Women* and starts reading ahead, even though Mr. Ripwinkle hates it when we do that.

I stare at her. The pre-Okalee's-death Helena would've stood beside me while I opened the envelope. It feels like this Helena is ignoring me.

"Are you okay?" I whisper again.

Kat walks into the classroom, and Lucia, and Wardie.

Helena glances up from her book. "Fine," she says with a quick smile.

Worry tugs at me, and I want to ask her more, but then Mr. Ripwinkle comes into class, face pale, eyes shadowed with gray like he didn't sleep well last night. *Me either, Mr. Ripwinkle,* I think.

He straightens his tie and says, "It's time for class to begin. Everyone please take your seats."

I make a mental note to talk to Helena at recess.

Wardie nods hello at me, and I nod back, my hand pasted over the card. Then, as Mr. Ripwinkle reads our morning poem, I open the envelope and scan the words.

> You still haven't explained why you lied. I saw you at the river with your sister right before she went under. Your secret is weighing on me. I want to tell someone, but first I need to know why you didn't tell the truth. I need to know why I saw what I saw. Maybe it's all a misunderstanding.
>
> If you write the truth down on a piece of paper and leave it on the top shelf of the back wall of the library between *World Book Encyclopedia Volume 1*

and *World Book Encyclopedia Volume 2* by
Friday at 12:00, I will consider how to
work this out with you. Otherwise I will
need to talk to an adult.

   That is the right thing to do. I have
kept quiet for too long already.

My fingernails turn white from pinching the card between them. I flip the card over. I look around the classroom for signs of guilt. Wardie's nodding along to Mr.
Ripwinkle's analysis of whatever poem he just read. Helena
is still buried in *Little Women*. Lucia Ang is yawning to
David Carter, like she thinks this class is boring.

   But Kat Waters is looking straight at me. And when I
meet her gaze, she doesn't look away. I hold the card up just
enough so she can see it and mouth the words, *Was this—*

   She whips back around before I can form a silent *you?*
on my lips.

   It must be her. She and I already talked in the library
once, so it makes sense that she'd want me to return there
with a declaration of truth. The librarian only comes a few
times a week, and in between the library is silent, books
gathering dust.

   I shiver. Note or no note, I *must* sing the solo this afternoon. And tomorrow I'll hide in the library and pounce on
Kat when she comes to get my paper. I'll get on my knees

and beg her to keep things quiet. To keep my secret between her and me alone.

I watch Kat nod along to Mr. Ripwinkle's lecture. My head feels light, too light. My vision tilts and shifts. I rest my forehead in my hands. How has it come to this—me depending on Kat's mercy to keep my world from sliding into the river, snagging and splitting against every rock and fallen tree on the way to the ocean?

It's unbearable to sit in class, listening to Mr. Ripwinkle drone on about a poem my eyes can't even focus on. I fold the note, hiding it in my palm. Then I get out of my desk and grab the bathroom pass off the wall. I need some air. But as I approach the door, I sense a shift in the classroom's atmosphere.

I turn around, ignoring Mr. Ripwinkle's glare. Kat is staring innocently at the whiteboard, but her white skin looks even paler than normal. Lucia is opening a piece of paper. She reads it, looks at me with real shock in her eyes, and slides it to Jessica Kline. Jessica reads the note, shoots me a pinched look of horror, and slides it onto David's desk. Only she isn't sneaky about it, and Mr. Ripwinkle stops what he's saying and frowns at David.

"What are you reading, Mr. Carter?"

The smooth brown skin of David's neck tightens. His curls tremble. David never gets in trouble, and now Mr. Ripwinkle has called him out in front of everybody because he's reading a note I'm almost one hundred percent sure is about me.

Kat has to have passed the note first. What did she write in it?

"Uh, I—" he stutters. Kat fidgets in her chair.

Mr. Ripwinkle holds his hand out. "Give it here."

Whatever it says, Mr. Ripwinkle *cannot* read that note.

I lunge toward David, bathroom pass clattering to the floor, and snatch the note from his outstretched fingers.

"Excuse me!" Mr. Ripwinkle roars. "I will not tolerate this—"

I sprint into the hallway. My shoes pound the tiles washed white by the fluorescent lights overhead. I bust out the front doors of the school. The cold air prickles my skin, and the wind howls and clouds squash the sky. I slink into the field and kneel on the damp earth.

Hands shaking, I unfold the note. In Kat's neat handwriting, it says:

> Yesterday, Phoebe practically confessed to me that she's keeping something secret about the way Okalee died. Something big! Let's meet after school. We have to convince Phoebe to tell us the truth so she and her parents—and all of us—can grieve and move forward.

My fist closes around a hunk of grass. I rip it out of the ground, bunch the note into a tight wad, and shove it in the hole. Then I scrape mud over the grave.

Kat doesn't care about Okalee. She definitely doesn't care about my parents.

She's pretending she cares about those things so no one will think she's a gossip who just wants the solo for herself. How can I stand in front of everyone in our community and sing if all my classmates—if my classmates' parents, like Wardie's father, who is a *police officer*—think I am a liar?

A strong wind whooshes through the grasses. *You* are *a liar. It's Kat who's telling the truth.*

I curl into a ball and stare at the strands of dead grass. The wind slams them down and lets them up, only to slam them down again. It starts to rain. I watch it puddle over the hole where I buried Kat's note. I know I can't stop the secret from spreading, not now that Lucia and Jessica and David know. How long will it take for the rumor to reach Mr. Ripwinkle? Dad?

Mamá?

A shiver courses through me. From somewhere in the tree line by the river comes the faint and mocking trill of a red-winged blackbird.

I leap up.

I have to stop this rumor.

I slam straight into Wardie as I turn the corner on my way back to the classroom.

"Phoebe?" He stares at me, probably wondering why I'm shivering and wet. "I was coming to—"

"I can't talk now, I have to—"

"Phoebe." Wardie glances over his shoulder to make sure no one's coming. "People are talking. They're saying you were with Okalee at the river right before she died."

I freeze. Then I sag against the cinder-block wall.

So they know already.

"I'm guessing that's what was in Kat's note?" Wardie takes off his jacket. He hands it to me, and I take it without thinking and hold it against me awkwardly.

"You put it on your shoulders," Wardie says, trying to smile.

Numb, I wrap the coat around my shoulders and wish I could disappear into it.

"Anyway, I know it's not true. Right?"

"Right," I croak.

Wardie nods. "I know you wouldn't lie about something like that."

I drop to the hallway floor. Why does Wardie think I'm so honest? *Because you always have been, until now.* Especially with Wardie.

"Besides," Wardie continues, crouching down with me, "I saw you in the river right after, searching. Okalee made her decision, and you did everything you could to find her." When I don't answer, he says my name again, urgent. "Phoebe."

I make myself meet his eyes.

"There's nothing more you could have done."

If only he knew about *involuntary manslaughter*. What an ugly word—*manslaughter*.

Wardie pats my shoulder, and even though he's touching me, I feel like we're so far away from each other, like I'm all alone at the top of stony Lone Peak, whipped by wind and snow, and he's here in the valley surrounded by warm foothills.

"Kat's just being Kat, you know? She wants that solo pretty bad, so she's playing all her cards to try to get it from you."

"The library thing, and now this," I say before remembering Wardie doesn't know about the card I opened right before Kat passed the note around about the rumor. She must've planned that after my visit to her house last night.

A thought stirs in the back of my mind. Why would Kat start a rumor if she promised to try to work it out with me at the library tomorrow at 12:00?

"What library thing?" Wardie says, and I have the feeling this is the second time he's asked this.

I pretend I don't hear him.

"She sang it yesterday after I left, didn't she?" I say hoarsely. "The solo."

He nods.

"Did it sound good?"

Wardie shakes his head. "It was fine. You know how Kat sings. But when you sang the solo last Friday, it was awesome. There's no way Kat should do it instead of you."

I duck my head so he won't see my face. My strange mixture of feelings is showing there right now, and I can feel all of it: joy, slim and brief; a huge shadow of sorrow; and, worst of all, the unmistakable edge of guilt.

I wish I deserved his praise. I wish I deserved his trust.

"I have to sing my solo today," I say.

"You can do it," Wardie says. "I believe in you."

"Hey, Wardie?"

"Yeah?"

"Do me a favor and tell Mr. Ripwinkle I had to see Dr. Santana, okay?"

He helps me to my feet. "Got it. I'll also tell people that rumor is baloney."

I look down at my shoes so he won't see the guilt in my eyes. After a moment I say, "Wardie?"

He smiles. "Yeah?"

"Thanks for coming to find me."

"Anytime." He gives me a brilliant Wardie smile and walks back to class. The feeling of Wardie's care warms me straight to my toes, a woodstove fire crackling against a winter night.

I wish everybody in the world could have a friend like Eduardo Mason.

The bell rings for a class change as I skitter into Dr. Santana's office. I slam the door shut behind me and rest my back against it, relieved to avoid the curious looks I know are coming my way now that Kat's rumor is out.

Dr. Santana looks up from her desk. A smile lights her face. "Phoebe! I'm glad you could—"

"Are my vocal chords broken?" I drop into an arm-chair. I feel bad for interrupting her, but I am running out of time. "Is that why I can't sing?"

"No," Dr. Santana says slowly. "If something was seriously wrong with your vocal chords, you wouldn't be able to talk at all."

I edge forward. "So why can't I sing? I've been doing the voice exercises Ms. Loring said would help with my singing. And I did them all just fine. But when I went to actually sing, all that came out was talking. Something is wrong with me, Dr. Santana. I cannot sing, and I need to sing this afternoon. And tomorrow. And especially Saturday night during the concert."

Dr. Santana rolls her chair around to the front of her

desk and sits directly across from me. The lavender candle flickers, illuminating her warm, dark eyes. "I think it has more to do with trauma, Phoebe, than with a physical ailment." She looks at me intently. "I've been thinking a lot about you and this singing issue, and I deeply believe that you'll need to do some hard work in order to move through the trauma and into grief. We have two months left of the school year, but I can arrange weekly sessions with you once summer starts."

Two months is too long. I need to move through the trauma now.

Through. Not past. What's it like, moving through trauma? I glance at the palm tree-shaped clock Dr. Santana has hung on the wall behind her desk. It's 10:30 a.m. I have less than four hours before I sing the solo.

I sit up straight. "Dr. Santana, I need to sing the solo today, not in two months. Please help me."

Dr. Santana gives me a sad half smile. "These things take time, Phoebe. Healing after a loved one dies is a process that continues for an entire lifetime."

I fold my hands together. "Please. Is there anything we could do to move through the trauma faster?"

Dr. Santana twists her lips. "Well," she says slowly, "I had something planned for a few weeks from now, but I suppose we could start it today."

"Thank you," I begin, but she holds up a finger.

"I'm not promising anything, Phoebe. Your singing voice will return when it's ready—when *you* are ready. But if you want to try to start processing your trauma, we can start the task of imaginal revisiting today." She lays a hand on my knee. "I'm afraid it won't be easy."

"Nothing in my life is easy anymore."

She nods. "That's true." She takes a small black device off her desk. "Okay. This is a voice recorder, and with it, we're going to start the very intense and very difficult work of revisiting the event of your trauma in your imagination."

My heart starts to pound. I wipe my hands on my jeans. "Didn't I do that on Wednesday?"

"You drew a memory, and it happened, I believe, to be of that day. But in order to process the trauma on an emotional level, you will speak it into this recorder. You and I will debrief by discussing what you've said. And then—and this part might be even harder than speaking it—you will listen to your voice tell the story."

I recoil. "No way."

"Let's slow down a bit, then. You can speak your story into the recorder, and then we will discuss what you've said. Then I will give the recorder to you, and you will put it in this box." She reaches behind her desk and draws out a fireproof safe. "Only I can access it. That means only I can access your recording."

I don't like any part of this supposed therapy. What good will it do to tell the story of what happened on River Day? I'm pretty sure Dr. Santana already guessed the truth from my drawing, and me saying it into a recording device makes it an out-loud, detailed, living thing.

Dr. Santana rests her hand on mine, and I flinch under the touch. "Remember, Phoebe, I have been through a very painful death too. I'm here to help you. I am on your side."

Just do the stupid therapy. Maybe it will make your singing voice come back.

"How do I know you won't show the tape to my mom and dad?"

Dr. Santana looks straight into my eyes. "Because I give you my word as a licensed professional counselor that I will not share your story with anyone, in any form, until you are ready."

"I'll never be ready." I feel almost hysterical. Am I really going to speak the truth into a little black piece of plastic? If I do, will I become myself again? Or will saying these things out loud make me even more of a stranger to myself? "Give me the recorder," I say, stretching out my hand.

Dr. Santana presses a button on it, and a green light starts blinking. She says, in the same low, soothing voice she uses all the time, "Phoebe, tell me about the moment you became aware of Okalee's death." She gives me a nod.

I swallow three times.

And then I begin.

12

I tell the recorder everything.

Almost everything, whispers a voice in the crook of my mind. There is something big I'm leaving out. Something my brain keeps editing in the flashbacks of that day. But I don't want to grab hold of that thing and draw it to the surface of my memory.

So I tell the recorder about River Day and how, the day before, Okalee announced that she would cross alone. How I told her that if she didn't hold my hand, we wouldn't do River Day. I leave out our fight there on the edge of the river, the way I tried to grab her. How she said I shoved her. That's too embarrassing. It makes me feel shameful. Why did our last real words to each other have to be a stupid fight?

I tell the recorder how I dove in after my sister, but it was too late. How I saw her surface once. Eyes closed, mouth open to the river pouring in. How I stood there, frozen.

Then I never saw her again.

And that, I tell Dr. Santana, was when I realized she was gone.

I hunch over the recorder, breathing hard and shallow breaths. Sorrow rises in my chest, its currents twisting and pushing against my throat. I turn the recorder off.

I look into Dr. Santana's empathetic face and say, "I let my sister drown, Dr. Santana." I can't bring myself to say, *I am guilty of manslaughtering my sister, Dr. Santana.*

"Oh, Phoebe." She takes hold of my hand, and its warm embrace promises me she won't tell any police officer what I've just said. "You must feel so much guilt. That is so, so difficult. Just breathe, and let yourself feel whatever's going through you. When you're ready, I want you to tell me how you felt as you told the story and relived your trauma."

I felt like someone's hands were coiled around my neck. I felt like I was drowning. I feel that way still.

Dr. Santana's voice flows through the room. "Breathe, Phoebe. Focus on the lavender scent, the warmth, the darkness."

"I felt guilty, like you said," I say finally. "I felt guilty and choking and sadder than I've ever felt in my whole entire life."

"And what about now? Looking back on the story from

an onlooker's perspective, we might say, what do you observe about the situation?"

My answer is swifter than the current that stole
Okalee. "I see the worst sister in the world."

I walk back to Mr. Ripwinkle's classroom after lunch
with a note from Dr. Santana tucked in my fist. Dr.
Santana didn't try to talk me out of any of my feelings.
She just had me write them down and tuck them in the
fireproof safe along with the tape recorder. She let me turn
the key, and I watched her store it in the zippered pocket
of her purse, which she assured me no one had access to
except for her.

I want to feel better now that I've told the story. But I
don't. The feelings that have hovered on the edges of my
consciousness since Saturday are trapped inside me now,
bobbing aimlessly through my bones.

I knock for Mr. Ripwinkle to let me in. I feel too dull,
heavy, and useless to care about the curious glances my
classmates give me as I enter the room. Mr. Ripwinkle
takes my note with a look of exasperation. He reads it,
then removes his glasses and rubs the bridge of his nose.
The class resumes their chatter. They're working on
group math, and soon they're paying no attention to Mr.
Ripwinkle and me.

"Are you all right?" he says gruffly.

I glance at him, surprised, and I nod.

"Are you?" I say, noticing the heaviness of his face. I'm surprised at myself. Since when do I care what prickly Mr. Ripwinkle is feeling? But I realize all of a sudden that Mr. Ripwinkle is a person with a life outside of school. And I have no idea what that life is like or what pain it might carry.

"I'm not, actually," Mr. Ripwinkle says. "But that can't be helped." He gives me a tired smile and nods for me to take a seat.

For a few minutes, I stare at Mr. Ripwinkle, who has resumed teaching our class like normal. I wonder what sorts of burdens everyone else in the world besides me is carrying.

Then the weight of my burden swings back and hits me in the chest, knocking the breath from my lungs.

In two hours I will stand on the stage in the gym, facing Okalee's empty chair, and attempt to sing my solo for Ms. Loring and the whole school to hear.

When the bell rings at two o'clock, my classmates shuffle their things into their backpacks, but I stay planted at my desk.

I hold completely still. I close my eyes and cover my

ears to shut out all the backpack-zipping noises. I try to feel the way I did before River Day: talented. Good at something. Beloved by my class and by my parents.

But I feel hollow and hated instead. A stone of dread sinks to the pit of my belly. I am empty, empty, empty, except for one hot, sick feeling that I can't name.

Is this how I will feel for the rest of my life?

By the time I open my eyes, almost everyone in the class has left.

"Coming?" Wardie says. I look around for Helena, but she's already gone.

Wardie and I step out the door and into the hallway. I walk slower than usual.

"So about the rumor," he says. "I told David it's a lie, and Jessica too. They seemed to believe me. But Lucia's another story. You know how she is with Kat."

I'm only half listening, partly because I'm nervous and partly because I'm scanning the mass of students for Helena. I spot her almost to the gym's double doors, talking to Kat. That's weird. Helena gently lays a hand on Kat's shoulder. Kat tries to keep walking, but then Helena's hand tightens. She tilts her head, shaking it slightly while saying something.

Kat stops cold. Her chin drops. Helena shakes her head again, her eyebrows firm and serious. The rest of the students part around them like a river current splitting around a boulder. Helena leans in to Kat again, and I can see her mouth moving, but I can't make out the words. Then she starts toward Wardie and me, leaving Kat to stare after her with a mixture of horror and confusion on her face.

Helena smiles at me. She rubs the pale skin of her neck. "You've got this, Phoebe," she says brightly. "Remember the thing we talked about? On the flyer? That's another reason to get your voice back."

"What thing?" Wardie says.

"Why were you talking to Kat?" I ask her. And why is she mentioning the *America's Voice* auditions? That was supposed to be a secret.

Helena smiles sadly. Now that she's so close, I realize she looks like she still has that headache from Wednesday. I wonder if Wardie feels unwell, too, after spending a whole afternoon defending a killer.

That sick feeling rises in me again, but this time I know exactly what it is.

Hatred.

I hate myself. More than Mamá ever could. The hatred rises like a beast in my chest, gulping me down from the inside out.

"Phoebe?"

I blink. Helena and Wardie are staring at me, worried. It's cold and gaping and horrifying inside my own head, so

I grab Helena's arm and sink my fingers into her flesh. She is my lifeboat.

"Are you okay?" she says, laying her hand over my fingers.

I relax them, just a little. If she knew the real me, if Wardie knew—

"I'm fine," I say. "Just nervous."

"I just told Kat off for spreading that rumor." She hooks her arm through mine. "I think she's always looked up to me a little. If anyone can make her shut up, it's me."

I should feel relieved, but the monster inside me is laughing, and I can barely breathe. Until this moment I didn't know that my classmates aren't my enemies.

They're not the people I should fear.

I am.

"Thanks, Helena," I manage to say.

"What flyer?" Wardie says again. "Sheesh, you guys are way too secretive."

I loop my elbow through Wardie's, trying to force the monster out by pretending I am fine, everything's fine. "I'll tell you later."

Ms. Loring ushers us all into the gym. "Welcome, welcome! Today we're going to practice the concert the way we will sing it on Saturday night, in tribute to Okalee Luz Petersen." She pauses and lets Okalee's full, beautiful name drift over us. A solemn hush swallows the gym until all I hear is my pounding heart and that awful laugh ringing in my bones.

She lines us up so that I am standing at the back of the stage, and everyone else is stretched out behind me. Cora Henry stands right behind me; she's giving a speech about Okalee, so she will also sing with the upper-grade choir. Ms. Loring said she's read Cora's tribute, but it's a surprise.

Wardie stands directly behind Cora because he's also giving a tribute.

The idea, Ms. Loring said, has changed a bit since she first thought of it. Instead of beginning with the solo right away, we will do this: the lights will be dark, our candles burning. Cora and Wardie and I will all have microphones. Out of the darkness, Cora's steady voice will speak her tribute to Okalee. And then Wardie's deepening, some-times-cracking voice will follow.

After that, we will observe a minute of silence to fill with prayers and thoughts about Okalee.

And then, after that deep and pure silence, my voice is supposed to rise into the night. A sister's tribute to a sister.

If only I can sing.

Kat's voice breaks into my trance. "Are you sure you can sing the solo, Phoebe? Ms. Loring, do you really think she should do it? What if she ruptures her vocal chords like Adele?"

I whip around. "This is for my sister, Kat. Of course

I can sing for her. Just give up trying to steal my solo already." I stand a little straighter even though everything inside me is crumpled. I think of my sister, and for the briefest second I see her, springy-haired and grinning. A feisty blackbird no one dared mess with.

Kat crosses her arms and gives me a little shrug that says, *I gave you a chance.*

I turn back around. I take slow breaths. I try not to think too much about how hard my heart is beating.

"I have confidence that Phoebe can do this, Kat." Ms. Loring gives me a thumbs-up and then jogs to the piano. "Hit the lights, David!"

The gym goes dark except for a low spotlight, just enough for Cora to read by.

Someone toward the back of the line begins to whisper, and someone else hisses for them to be quiet.

Cora clears her throat. "She was named for the red-winged blackbird, for the sound that bird makes. And like the trilling call of her namesake bird, Okalee was vibrant. She was soulful. She cared. Her middle name was Luz, which means *light* in Spanish. Okalee was a light to me.

"My name is Cora Henry. I am a member of the Chippewa Cree Tribe, but I grew up here in Grayling Crossing, pretty far away from a lot of my Chippewa Cree family and friends in Rocky Boy.

"Sometimes it's been really hard because the colonizers

who've been coming to Montana since the 1800s just decided that this was their land, even though there were
plenty of people on it already. Lots of us had been pushed
away from our original homes, but we made a new home
here. And even then, people still try to erase our existence.
But we've been here all along. Whenever I told Okalee
about something hurtful someone said, she just listened.
Some people try to tell me I shouldn't feel bad, that words
are just words, but Okalee didn't do that. She always listened to me.

"One of the reasons Okalee and I became friends is because we both love words. About a year ago, we both got
really interested in poetry, which is how we ended up going
to a poetry reading at Montana State University this past
winter.

"That's where we first heard a poem called 'Remember'
by Georgeline Morsette, a student at MSU who is
Chippewa Cree too. Okalee and I both loved the poem so
much that we made a goal to memorize it. We both know
the first lines by heart:

> *When you feel afraid, remember;*
> *Where one tree falls, more can grow.*
> *Even though sometimes it's hard to let go*
> *Everything pushes and pulls for a reason.*
> *Everything changes, just like the seasons."*

I let those words wash through me again. If only I knew how to be like a new tree, growing strong out of something terrible.

Cora clears her throat. "Okalee wanted to become a pediatric nurse, but she was afraid it would be too hard. I have fears about becoming a successful artist, painter, and poet. I don't know if I'm talented enough. Every time Okalee felt her fears crowding up inside her, she would ask me to say the first lines of the poem out loud. And when I felt like becoming an artist was impossible, Okalee would recite those words to me."

Cora continues to read off her paper. "A couple days before she died, Okalee said being ten didn't make things impossible for us. She said age was just a number, that we could start growing our talents and strengths right away."

My mind flashes back to Okalee on River Day. *I am not a little girl. I can cross alone. Watch me.*

"She said you didn't have to be grown up to spread beauty in your world. Okalee and me, we inspired each other. She said that no matter how old she got, if she ever felt like becoming a nurse was too hard, she would imagine me saying the words from 'Remember' in her head."

Cora pauses. "Now I have to say those words out loud to myself, alone, every time fear tries to choke me. Which is a lot these days. But I keep saying those words. I say them for me. And I say them for my sister-friend, Okalee Luz Petersen."

I never knew Okalee was afraid of anything. She always seemed braver than me. Incapable of being nervous.

Did I even know my sister?

Silence follows. And then Wardie speaks. "Wow. She would've loved that, Cora."

I turn around and open my arms. Cora drops into them, small and soft and quaking. "You really loved each other, didn't you?" I whisper into her hair.

"I still love her," she whispers back, standing beside me and leaning her head against my shoulder.

"Thank you so much, Cora," Ms. Loring says. I can tell she's been crying. "Wardie? You're next."

Wardie steps to the front of the stage and talks about how Okalee was like a little sister to him, how he loved to show her fox dens and birds' nests and how she loved to take him to the Wood of the Eyes and play hide-and-go-seek among the all-knowing eyes of the aspen trunks. I realize, while Wardie speaks, that he must be grieving Okalee as much as I am. Have I even noticed? Have I even acknowledged that to him?

When he finishes, I reach for Wardie and grab his hand. My throat feels too full of nerves and the unasked *How are you feeling, Wardie?* and sorrow, and I can't speak. I squeeze his hand twice.

I'm sorry, I say through those squeezes. I hope he understands.

He squeezes me firmly back and then lets go.

"Okay, Phoebe." Ms. Loring plays my opening notes. "Let's say the minute of silence has passed now. This is where you come in."

The students toward the back of the line have started talking quietly. Ms. Loring shushes them. The talking stops.

I take a deep breath, bracing myself against the stabbing feeling in my lungs. I close my eyes.

I bring the wire mesh of the microphone to my lips. Thrills of nervousness shoot into my belly. The velvet darkness shifts against my skin. I close my eyes and imagine a crowd full of people watching, waiting, for me to sing. I pretend Mamá hasn't forbidden me from singing this very solo. I imagine her sitting in the audience, smiling as she listens to me sing for my sister. Dad would be proud for sure.

If only he would convince Mamá that I need to do this. If only they'd come.

"Phoebe," Cora whispers when I don't say anything. "Do you want me to say it for you? The poem?"

I nod and reach behind me to squeeze Cora's hand. She sends the words my way, soft and quiet, and they reach into the cracked, dry places in my soul where Okalee's absence hurts the most.

Ms. Loring plunks out my opening note again. *When you feel afraid, remember; Where one tree falls, more can grow.* I must sing this, or else Ms. Loring will give the solo to Kat. I must prove to myself that I can do this singing thing, that I can sing now and at the concert the day after tomorrow at the Grayling Crossing Inn, that I can sing before the *America's Voice* judges.

I have to sing because if I don't, it'll prove that there's nothing of *me* left to grab on to. That everything that made me *me* got wiped out when I let Okalee go into that river. When I lied.

Silence gathers in the space after the piano's last echo. Now is my time. I take a deep breath and think of the hard work I did this morning with Dr. Santana, how I started moving through the trauma. How I told someone the truth. I focus on the sweet, sheltering darkness and on the way I know I will feel once the song spills from my lips.

"As I went down in the river to pray," I begin. Rust laces my voice, but I'm doing it, I'm finally singing!

Kat giggles from her spot behind me. Someone else whispers, "Yikes."

I won't listen to them. I pinch my eyes shut and take a good swallow, imagining oil pouring down my throat and smoothing the rust away.

Studying about that good old way
And who shall wear the starry crown
Good Lord, show me the way.

My voice can't seem to rise above a rusty singing whisper, but as the spotlight on me slowly grows brighter, a thrill runs through my bones. That feeling like the first September snow drifting to earth slips past the thrill and unfurls into the rest of me.

Maybe I'm still here after all.

Maybe I'm still me.

"That's it, Phoebe," Wardie says. "You got this."

Yes. Yes. I will my voice to rise above a whisper. I will it to flow out of me, unrestrained.

But then hot, burning words tiptoe into my ears. Shocked whispers move through the crowd.

"Are you for real?" David whispers.

"Someone saw her *push* Okalee into the river?" says Lucia.

My eyes fly open.

"With her hands?" says Jessica Kline.

"Yes, with her hands, what else?"

Kat.

"Why would she do something like that?" Cohen asks.

"You wanna ask?" Kat. Horrible, selfish Kat.

"No way. You do it."

Alarm is sounding a warning in my body, and the hope of the last few moments is gone. The song dies as soon as it's out of my mouth. It's husky and flat, not a song at all.

I swivel around. Wardie and Cora are facing Kat, taking in this new information. Ms. Loring calls out, "What's going on?"

Helena's mouth hangs open, her freckles popping even in the low glare of the spotlight. Pretty much everyone else in the upper grades has the same expression on their faces. It takes me two seconds to find the blonde bob, the too-bright eyes.

Kat looks smug and triumphant, and that's when I know she is, without question, the pink-hoodie girl who saw us at the river that day, who wrote the note to me. Who's been tormenting me ever since Okalee drowned.

Cora tugs on my hand. "They're saying you pushed Okalee in," she says. Her face is open and concerned. She's begging me to deny it.

I'm yanked back to the river's edge, to the pebbles clawing into my feet and the sun glaring on the water. Okalee's face is bunched up in anger. *I am not a little girl.*

It's as though I'm watching myself in a movie. I see a girl with my curly, dark hair and a look of desperation on her face.

"Seriously, Okalee, you have to hold my hand."

She grabs for her sister's elbow, but Okalee wrenches

her arm away so hard she twists and falls forward. Her chin skims the river, but she catches herself and stands up straight.

"Don't shove me!"

I failed Okalee in almost every way but one.

I didn't shove her. I didn't.

I plow through the line of shocked faces.

Kat has turned away from me, but I close my hand over her shoulder and jerk her back around. I feel big and ugly. "What did you do?" I yell in her face. "What did you say to them?"

"Phoebe!" Wardie tugs on my shoulders.

"I didn't push her in. Why would you say that?" I shake Kat as hard as I can. Her chin rattles. Spit drops from her lips.

Wardie tugs harder, yanking me away from Kat.

Kat breathes hard. She looks like a deer about to get eaten by a grizzly. The rest of my classmates back away from me slowly.

"Why don't you all just play dead then?" I shout. "If you're so scared of me, do it. Lie down. Play dead."

I want to stop, but I can't. My mouth, my mouth that almost sang, keeps shouting.

"You think I killed her? You think I pushed my own sister into the river? Well, you're all idiots. You're all wrong. I can't believe you would ever think that."

"Phoebe. Phoebe!" Ms. Loring takes my elbow. "Come over here, sweetheart. Come on, now. Wardie, can you— yes, thank you. Helena, some water, please?"

They sit me down on a metal chair. The cold of it seeps through my jeans and spreads into my skin until I am a frozen, empty blob.

"I'll call your parents," Ms. Loring says to me.

"No!" I grab Ms. Loring's hand. "Please don't call them." If they know about this, they will never let me sing on Saturday, and now that's my last chance to find myself. To find Okalee.

Ms. Loring looks at me with pity in her eyes. "Oh, Phoebe."

"Please." Horror seizes me. If Mamá and Dad come here, they will hear what set me off. They will hear the words *someone saw Phoebe push Okalee into the river*. And if they hear that, they will demand to hear the full story.

Ms. Loring looks helplessly at Wardie, and he kneels down in front of me. "Hey, Phoebe. Wanna get out of here?"

All eyes are pinned on me. Whispers rush like river water. I nod.

Wardie waits for me to stand up and follow him. We walk past Helena and her cup of water. Wardie takes it and murmurs something to her.

He leads me outside, where Bo is grazing in the back

field and the blue-tinged mountains push toward a gray sky. Wardie says nothing. He just sits down on a rock, and I sit too, breathing in his safe scent. Fresh tortillas. Old books. Pine needles.

I wonder what I smell like. Stone? Wind? A howling emptiness?

"Phoebe," he says after a few minutes have passed. "I've been thinking."

A breath of wind whooshes through the grasses.

"I've been thinking about Okalee." He pauses. "I know I said I thought you'd never lie. That I believed your story of what happened."

The grasses hold still.

"But your face in there . . ." A shiver passes from Wardie to me. "I don't know. You know you can tell me anything, right?"

I stare at the details of the grasses: their blade edges, their yellow color, the way the wind wrestles them down but they get back up again and again.

A few months ago, Mr. Ripwinkle's morning poem was one by Robert Frost. It was one of the few that stuck with me, though I never knew why.

> *Two roads diverged in a yellow wood,*
> *And sorry I could not travel both*

And be one traveler, long I stood
And looked down one as far as I could.

I never understood what it meant, even though Mr. Ripwinkle and Helena and David got into an energetic discussion about it that took up the entire English period one day.

But I understand it now. In my yellow wood, there are three roads, not two, and the third isn't even blazed yet. It's a tangle of evergreens and underbrush and truth, and if I start up it, I must take a hatchet to the lie that's hollowing out my chest.

I know if I take a road already forged, I will lose Wardie.

I can't look at him. "You won't like me if I tell you the truth."

Wardie's quiet. He swallows, like he's nervous to hear what I'm about to say. But then he says, "I'm never not going to be your friend."

I force myself to meet his gaze. I look at the worry lines creasing his brown forehead and the corners of his beautiful brown eyes.

I squeeze my fingers together, take a deep breath, and make myself begin. You'd think telling a mental health professional would be scarier than telling my best friend, but with Wardie, I have more to lose. "Okalee and I had a tradition. We called it River Day, and it was secret. No one else in the whole world knows about it. Except Dr. Santana, because I told her just this morning. It was my invention. I started it when I was nine and she was seven. It was supposed to celebrate spring coming to the Gallatin Valley."

I leave out the part about how it was my own way of proving that I was better than her, braver than her. There are some things nobody else, not Okalee or Dr. Santana or anyone, needs to know.

"Basically, on River Day, Okalee and I held hands and crossed the river. That first time, the river wasn't that high." I look down, but I can feel Wardie's eyes on me. "But this year . . ." I swallow hard. What will Wardie, ranger-in-training, say? "It was the snowmelt river, Wardie. It was so high I couldn't even see the boulder in the middle."

He shakes his head just a little, and he doesn't have to say anything. I know what's going on in his mind. Crossing the river when it's that high? A stupid, stupid mistake. A greenhorn mistake. But he says nothing, and I'm glad.

"My parents were at my Great-Aunt Astrid's. They had no idea what we were going to do. As soon as they left, Okalee and I went down to the river."

My heart starts pounding.

"The day before, she'd said she was going to cross by herself. But I told her no way. I told her if she did that we wouldn't have River Day at all. And so she promised she would hold my hand, like always. But then, on Saturday, she distracted me. She told me to look at some red-winged blackbirds, and I did, and while I was looking, she went in. I followed her and I tried to grab her, but she snatched her hand away and fell deeper into the river. She shouted, 'Don't shove me!' But I didn't shove her. I was trying to keep her with me."

Wardie is still so quiet, and the silence batters my temples. I want him to talk. To say something, anything.

Finally Wardie touches my hand lightly. Just for a second, like a butterfly landing and departing in one breath. "Phoebe," he whispers. "That's the worst."

He doesn't hate me. I take a big breath and keep talking. "I watched her get to the boulder," I say, words tripping over each other in an effort to get out. "And then I saw how much trouble we were in because she looked so tiny in that water. I yelled for her to stop and come back, that I was coming to help her. She glanced over her shoulder, and she took her hand off the boulder, and then she went under. I saw her come up once. Her eyes were closed. Then the river yanked her back under, and I never saw her alive again."

That's not the whole truth, Phoebe, my cruel mind whispers, but already I'm shaking, I'm sweating.

"That's the truth," I say softly. *No, it's not*, says that voice, but I pinch it so hard it slinks, flattened, into the marrow of my bones. "The rumor isn't a rumor. It's true."

The sun elbows out from behind the clouds and then,

just as quickly, hides behind them again. A long shadow shifts over the field.

"Phoebe." Wardie wriggles so his face is right in front of mine. His eyes are wide and serious. "You didn't push her in. You didn't make her die. Okalee was the most independent person I've ever known."

I try to speak, but my voice slips and falls. *Steady, Phoebe.* I try again. "Maybe I didn't kill her, but I ignored the voice in my head that told me she might do something like that. I should have canceled River Day. I should have fought her harder when she went in or—"

"Phoebe." Wardie shakes his head. "Don't do that to yourself." He shrugs helplessly. "She's gone." His voice tilts up when he says this, like it's a statement and a question and a tragedy all at once.

An ugly sound curdles my voice, and my face crumples. I paste my hands over my eyes as the sobs take over. And Wardie hesitates for a moment, but then he curls both his arms around my shoulders, and he's all bony elbows and awkward spaces, and we rock like that from side to side until we settle into a rhythm soft as a boat riding the gentle waves of a crystal lake.

13

Wardie and I walk slowly around the school. I'm
telling him about involuntary manslaughter and
"Montana Code Annotated 45-7-205: False reports to law
enforcement authorities" and about the typed-up notes
when I catch a glimpse of a dark-green truck in the parking lot.

The 4Runner. I don't know how I didn't hear it pull in.

"No," I gasp. I run to the front doors of the school.
"No, no, no—"

Wardie follows right behind me. We open the glass
double doors, and there they are, Dad almost as tall as the
ceiling, Mamá tiny next to him. They are facing away from
me, which is a good thing because when I realize what
Mamá is wearing, what she looks like under the harsh hallway lights, I can't move.

She's wearing the same plaid pajama pants she put on

after Okalee's funeral. They hang loose around her waist. Her black curls are stuffed into a tangled bun. A stained T-shirt clings to her shoulders. I can smell her from here: hair clumped with grease, skin unwashed, teeth sweatered with yellow bacteria. Her hand is neatly wrapped in a white bandage—the only neat thing about her. Dad must've insisted on keeping her burns clean.

It's as though I'm not looking at my mother at all. I miss her so fiercely that my fists knot up at my sides. I want this impostor Mamá to go away. I want my warm, black-currant-and-vanilla-smelling Mamá back. I want the Mamá who nags me about schoolwork, who sews me aprons, who bakes with me every day after school, who fills the kitchen with the aromas of black beans and ropa vieja and tostones.

The gym doors swing open, and my classmates file out, some of them stopping and staring at my parents. Principal Flores is talking to them, her hand on Mamá's T-shirt as though nothing's wrong. She's gesturing toward Dr. Santana's office.

"Phoebe went out for some fresh air with Wardie, but they'll be back any minute now . . ." I hear her say.

"Mamá." I take a step forward.

Mamá turns around. Her face is the gray of dirty snow during the spring thaw.

"Phoebe." She sounds so tired. "What happened?"

I speak Spanish so that no one—except Dad, Wardie, and maybe Principal Flores—will understand. "¿Por qué estás vestida así?" I know I shouldn't say anything about how Mamá is dressed. I know she's drowning in her pain. But with Mamá looking like that, and all the attention that's on me already—it's too much.

Dad shakes his head. "Phoebe, let it go." His flannel shirt is buttoned all the way up to his Adam's apple. His jeans are clean and blue. He smells of aftershave and Dove soap.

"Why can't you be more like Dad?" I say to my mother, desperate.

Mamá blinks. The hollowness of her face gets worse, and I know I shouldn't have said that. But I don't know how else to get my real Mamá back.

Kat Waters walks by. She stares at Mamá, a hint of revulsion on her face. She glances at me and narrows her eyes. Her shirt collar is still crooked from when I shook her. I look away, embarrassed. I feel like a schoolyard bully. Since when did I start shaking people and ordering them to do what I want?

Helena scampers past like she doesn't even know Mamá and Dad and me, and I suddenly feel furious at her, at Mamá, at everything and everyone.

"Hey!" I shout after her. "Wardie's here with me. Where have you been, Helena?"

She stops walking. She turns around. "I'll talk to you later, I promise. I'm—"

"Go to class, Miss McClain," Principal Flores says. "Phoebe, please try to calm down."

But I can't calm down. There's a river rushing through my head, drowning all my reason. Filling my mind with grit. Smashing my thoughts against my skull.

Then Dr. Santana opens the office door and says, "Phoebe." Her voice is an anchor. I meet her eyes, relieved to have someone to hold on to.

But then I realize that Mamá and Dad are about to enter my safe place, where I spoke the truth into a recorder. They're about to find out I'm still going through with singing the solo.

They're about to find out what I did to Okalee.

The adults usher me inside. My hands are still closed into fists. The river in my head is rushing, rushing. "Can Wardie stay? Please?"

"I'm afraid not. Wardie needs to go back to class." Principal Flores thanks him for his help and shoos him away, and I am left in the office with Mamá, Dad, Principal Flores, and Dr. Santana.

Mamá takes it all in, her gaze snagging on the Honor Jar. She reaches inside and wraps her hand around Okalee's rock. She bites her lip.

I want to say *Let go of that! You aren't my mother—you*

can't touch that. But she *is* my mother, of course she is, and she's tainting my angry sorrow with hers that won't let her bathe or brush her teeth or put on some clean clothes.

"What's going on?" Dad says.

"Take a seat, Mr. Petersen." Dr. Santana motions for him and Mamá to take the armchairs. She points me to her rolling chair and leans against her desk. Principal Flores stands by the door.

I drop into the chair. Dad folds his giant hands together and looks earnestly at Dr. Santana and then at me. Mamá slides Okalee's rock between her fingers, tears shining in her eyes.

She looks thin and small and sad, and I want to reach out and touch her, but my hands are frozen with anger. I've never felt this clash of anger and guilt and missing before, not ever in my life.

I miss Okalee. I miss Mamá. I miss the life I had before River Day.

Principal Flores rubs her collarbone and blows out a breath. "Phoebe acted out violently during choir practice today. She shook another girl by the shoulders— quite hard, I might add—and it scared our other students. Phoebe has a solo for the concert on Saturday, but we're concerned about her behavior."

Mamá drops the rock in her lap. "She is forbidden from singing that solo."

I grip the seat. The anger in me takes over. *Petersen girls love a challenge*, I think. And this is a challenge I have to win.

"You never said forbid, Mamá. You just said you didn't want me to."

Dr. Santana kneels in front of Mamá. "It's been hard. I imagine this week has been excruciating for you, Mrs. Petersen. Ha sido terrible." She holds her hands out for Mamá, and Mamá clings to them, a ghost of a smile at Dr. Santana's flawless Spanish. The ghost disappears so fast I'm not sure it ever was there. She nods quickly and uses her shoulder to wipe away a stream of tears.

Dad puts his hand on Mamá's shoulder. "We're just worried that it's all too much, too soon. Phoebe's having issues with her—"

"I don't have any issues," I butt in, casting Dad a glance that says *please, not a word about my voice*. I don't want Principal Flores to tell Ms. Loring I'm still struggling.

Dad's shoulders drop. "We're just not sure Phoebe's ready for such a big commitment."

Dr. Santana turns to me. She's still holding Mamá's hands. "How do you feel about the solo, Phoebe?"

I think of the way I felt when I whisper-sang this afternoon.

"If I can't sing the solo, I feel like I'll . . ." I search for the right word. "Dissolve. Like I won't be able to hold myself together anymore."

Dr. Santana gives me a sad smile. She looks at Mamá. "And you, Mrs. Petersen. How would you feel?"

"Call me Soledad," Mamá says softly.

"How would you feel, Soledad?" Dr. Santana says.

Mamá's lips press tight together. "Angry," she whispers. "I would feel very, very angry. Estoy asustada . . ."

"You're scared," Dr. Santana says quietly. "You're scared of feeling that angry?"

Mamá nods. "Yes."

Why would Mamá feel so mad? Because I couldn't sing at Okalee's funeral?

Dr. Santana looks at Dad. "And how do you feel, Mr. Petersen?"

"Lars," Dad says with a small smile. Then he takes a deep breath. "I feel torn. On the one hand, I understand Phoebe's need to sing. And on the other, I get where Soli's coming from." He shrugs, biting his bottom lip. I've never seen him do that before.

He's trying not to cry.

I hug myself tight. Dr. Santana nods at Principal Flores. "Okay. I'm glad I understand where everyone's coming from. Now, before we talk more about the solo, I believe we have some disciplinary issues to discuss."

Principal Flores looks at Mamá and Dad. "When we

got down to the roots of the story, it seems Phoebe's assault was set off by some rumors that are circulating concerning the manner in which Okalee died. The girl Phoebe assaulted was the one whispering these rumors, and she's admitted this, though she won't say where she heard them."

Mamá leans forward. Her knuckles turn milky.

My legs jitter and jump.

"What's the rumor?" Dad asks slowly.

Principal Flores exchanges a glance with Dr. Santana. "Well, Mr. Petersen, kids are saying that someone saw Phoebe and Okalee at the river together before Okalee drowned . . . and someone has now spread the rumor that Phoebe pushed Okalee in."

Mamá jerks around to face me. She breathes hard. She opens and closes her mouth. Then finally she gasps, "I knew it." She presses her fingers to her pale face. Splotches of red creep up her neck. Her voice goes low and hard. "I knew something wasn't right."

She's never talked to me in that voice before, and it shakes me harder than I shook Kat.

"It's not true!" I leap up. "It's a rumor, Mamá. I told you the truth on Saturday. I swear."

Dad reaches his hand out to me, and I take it. He envelops my fingers in his, and it's like I'm leaning against the wood-shavings scent of his flannel shirt. "Sit down,

Phoebe," he says kindly. "It's all right. No one's blaming you for anything."

Mamá shakes her head. "I knew it, I knew it, I knew it."

"Soledad," Dad says, a warning note in his voice.

Mamá stands up. She reaches out and grabs my chin with her trembling, sweating fingers. "Tell me the truth. Tell me how my daughter died."

That horrible hardness is still there in her voice. A wall springs up between us. Though her fingers are touching my face, my mother and I have never been further apart in our lives.

Tell me how my daughter died.

Would I still be Mamá's daughter if she knew? Would she ever hand me a spoon to scoop cookie dough with after school while she whistled her jazzy tune? Would she ever lean against me, her warm shoulder cozying into mine, and ask me how my day went?

And Dad. Would he ever again take me to Ennis Lake to listen to the haunting call of a common loon? Or ask me to go for an evening walk along the river to watch out for kingfishers and American dippers in the spring?

I look directly at Mamá. I pray that my features look straight and true. I pray that Mamá does not look too deep into my liar-green eyes.

I say, "I already told you the truth."

I say, "Okalee went in the river all by herself and drowned."

I say, "I wasn't there to help her."

Dr. Santana's eyes are on me, but I can't look at her. If I do, I might shatter.

Mamá drops her hand. She slumps back into her chair. "Okay, Phoebe," she says quietly.

I can't tell if she believes me or not. All I know is her voice sounds softer now, gentler. Resigned.

All at once I feel exhausted and aching, and I know I have to get out of there. I scoot toward the door.

"Where are you going?" Dad says.

I push past Principal Flores.

Dr. Santana says, "We're not done—"

I shut the door and sprint outside. Mamá's silence is loud behind me. She didn't try to keep me back.

Wardie's at my side in a millisecond. Relief sweeps through me. "I couldn't make myself go back to class," he says. "Are you okay?"

"We need to get out of here." I run out the door, Wardie's footsteps smacking the floor behind me.

↟ ↟ ↟ ↟

We sprint deep into the forest on Wardie's side of the river. The branches of firs and spruces slap my face. Angry tree roots rise out of the ground and trip me. Finally I collapse against a fallen log and gasp breath back into my lungs. Wardie flops down next to me.

"I can't be around them," I say. "My mom doesn't believe me, but I can't tell her the truth. I can't tell her I was there when Okalee went into the river." Desperation chokes my voice. That's not all I can't say about that day. "If she knew, she would hate me. My dad would too. And if the police—if *your* dad—finds out, I'll go to jail."

The hopelessness of my situation curls its fingers around my throat.

"My dad wouldn't send you to jail."

"He'd have to. It's the law."

Wardie blows a hard breath. "We're in a crappy situation."

We. I'm not alone. I have Wardie. I feel warm all over, and the fingers loosen a tiny bit.

I turn to him. "Can I stay at your house tonight?"

Wardie's eyes widen. "Sure."

"Do you think your dad will ask me about the rumor?"

Wardie shakes his head. "Nah. When he's off duty, he's off duty."

I think of Wardie's family, his mami and dad who bake and cook and take showers.

"I hate being home," I say quietly. "There's this heavy fog that won't ever go away. It's cold and damp, and it clings to your mind. My mom doesn't shower or even brush her teeth. And my dad's so helpless, like he doesn't know what to do to make her better or to make our life half-normal again. Our house is a mess, and every time I walk by Okalee's room, I just want to run in and tell her about it, but then I remember." I lean my head on the rough skin of the log. "They've got to let me still sing the solo."

Wardie settles his elbow on the log and rests his head on his hand. I know he understands everything I've left unsaid. I can smell the urgency of me the way I could smell the grime of Mamá. It smells like a girl trying to break away from a racing river, like a skier trying to escape an avalanche that's barreling down a mountainside. It feels as though there's no way I will be able to sing on Saturday night or ever again in my life.

"Hey." Wardie touches my arm, and my skin prickles with attention. "You did kind of sing today. It sounded nice."

"But then the song went away."

Wardie sits up, leans forward. He plucks a piece of bark off the log and rubs it nervously between his hands. "Do you think maybe you can't sing because of the . . . you know, the lie?"

I drop my hands away from my face.

Could it be that easy, and could it be that hard?

"I don't think that's it," I say. "I think it's just a big combination of everything."

But then a breeze drops the lace scarf of its breath over the back of my neck, and I shiver and wonder if he is right. If I need to tell the truth not just to Wardie and to Dr. Santana, but to Dad. To Mamá.

To everyone.

But if I do that, I won't be able to sing the solo because I'll be at the police station instead of at the Grayling Crossing Inn, waiting to get booked into jail or whatever it is that happens to people who commit manslaughter.

Wardie tosses the bark back into the mud. "I don't know, then."

"I have to sing, Wardie," I say. "Remember when you said Helena and I were too secretive? Well, there's this other thing I want to sing for. I haven't told anybody about it yet. It's an audition. An *America's Voice* audition. It's at the Gallatin Valley Mall in a couple weeks, and the winner of the contest gets to go to Los Angeles to audition for the real show."

Wardie raises his eyebrows. "That's awesome. You could totally win it. I know you could."

"That's what Helena said too," I say softly. "She's the one who showed me the flyer. But she hasn't mentioned it since Okalee . . . you know."

Pain flashes through Wardie's eyes, and I think of his speech about Okalee. I study his face and realize he looks both older and younger than he did before River Day.

"You know, Wardie, I really loved your tribute. I'm sorry I haven't asked you this before, but . . . how are *you?*"

Wardie clears his throat. "It's rough." His voice sounds like sandpaper. "I can't believe she's gone. I miss hearing her run across the bridge to ask me about animal tracks. I miss hearing her chatter in the kitchen. Did you know she'd talk with Mami and they'd write poetry together sometimes? I miss seeing her wave at me from across the river." He stops talking and looks away. "And I feel like if I'd have gotten there sooner, maybe I could've stopped both of you from going in. Or maybe I could've scooped her out of the water or something. You know?"

I try to keep my face from showing surprise. I had no idea Wardie felt guilty too.

"I know Helena and I don't miss her as much as you do," Wardie says, "but we really miss her. Remember how Okalee loved to ride with Helena on Bo?"

I smile. Helena always let Okalee ride with her if the ground was dry and there wasn't a chance of Bo slipping and throwing Okalee. How could I forget that Helena loved Okalee too?

"I've only been thinking of myself," I say quietly.

Wardie gives me a sad half smile. "No one blames you for that. She was your blood."

She was my blood. My blood, who I betrayed.

Only two days until I must sing. Two days until the lie won't matter anymore.

Because surely Mamá will eventually forget her doubts. Surely, as time passes, they'll erode like the edge of a silty, rocky riverbank.

14

oments after Wardie and I ease into his quiet, clean house, a soft knock sounds on the front door.

I know that knock. I square my shoulders and open the door. Dad stands before me, hands in his pockets. I'm relieved not to see Mamá standing next to him. And if I'm honest with myself, I'm disappointed too.

"Thought I might find you here," Dad says.

"Come in, Mr. Petersen," Wardie calls from behind me.

"That's all right. I'll just be a minute." Dad rubs his blond stubble. "Your mom was pretty upset, Phoebe. She left just after you did. Walked into town to get some air, try to relax."

I cringe to think of Mamá, dressed the way she is, walking through downtown Grayling Crossing. Then I feel ashamed.

"I talked to the principal and the counselor for a long

time," Dad continues, "and we've decided to let you make the decision about singing on Saturday night."

A sharp thrill of nerves and joy shoots into me, lifting me to my tiptoes. "Really? Does Mamá know?"

"No." Dad presses his fingers to his temple. "She doesn't. And she's not going to be happy with me when she finds out. But I'll try to convince her. And no matter what, I will be there to hear you. I promise. Principal Flores wants you to stay home tomorrow to reflect on your actions, get some rest, and write a letter apologizing to Kat, Ms. Loring, and your classmates for the disruption you've caused. You're also going to do a week of detention starting next week."

"I can do that," I say. "Thanks, Dad."

"Are you staying here tonight?" he says, nodding at the Masons' house.

Wardie's loading firewood into their woodstove. The Masons' dog, Bunny, bounds over to him and licks his ear. He laughs and pushes her away.

Once again someone close to me has surprised me with how deep their understanding goes. "I need to get away," I say. What I don't say is *From Mamá and the hardness in her voice.* "Just till the concert's over." I also have a sliver of fear that if I'm home this weekend, Mamá will lock me in my room on Saturday night so that I can't go to the concert.

"I understand. I'll miss you, my girl, but I understand."

I lean into his soft flannel shirt, and he wraps his strong arms around me, and then he starts to shake and I realize he's weeping. "I love you so much," he whispers, shoulders hitching.

The first time I ever saw Dad cry was at the riverbank the day Okalee drowned. That time, I ran from the sight.

Today, though, I hug him close. He clings to me, and I cling back.

After a minute, he pulls away and draws his sleeve across his face. "I better go find your mother." He kisses my cheek. A mourning dove *hoo-hoos* from somewhere near the rushing river.

Dad walks away. I close my eyes to savor the feeling of my father loving me, trusting me. Because I know that if he knew the real me, if he knew my lie, he would do neither.

⌁ ⚹ ⌁ ⚘

"It's wonderful to have you here, Phoebe." Mrs. Mason hands me a basket filled with warm tortillas. Wardie slides the butter dish my way. Officer Mason—Mr. Mason—nods in agreement. He changed out of his uniform and into his normal Mr. Mason clothes as soon as he got home, and I don't feel afraid that he'll suddenly figure out the truth and arrest me.

Mr. Mason ladles albondigas into my bowl, the beef meatballs in chicken-tomato broth tantalizing even my knotted stomach. "How've you been holding up, Phoebe?"

I blow on a spoonful of soup. I almost say *I'm fine*, but that's not true. Something about the Masons is so genuine and honest. Flames dance against the glass of the woodstove door. Every few minutes, the fire snaps cheerily, glowing brighter for that instant. Mr. Mason had put a Nickel Creek CD into his speaker system before supper, and now the sounds of banjos and violins pours through me like warm tea.

It's cozier than Dr. Santana's office in here. Painfully cozy compared to my house.

"I'm hanging in there," I say finally.

Mrs. Mason reaches across the table and squeezes my hand. She's been visiting Mamá every day, just sitting with her sometimes. She always brings food, and Mamá nibbles at it, which is more than she does with all those casseroles still in the fridge.

Mr. Mason nods understandingly. But I don't want to talk about me. So I say, "How have you guys been?"

The Masons exchange smiles.

"Well, Phoebe, your sister has changed my life, let me tell you." Mr. Mason puts his napkin down and folds his hands. "I'm tired of being a cop. Throwing people in jail is trying to fix the problem without acknowledging its roots.

So I'm going to start a program in Bozeman for kids of parents in homeless shelters, kids on the streets. I'm still going to work as an officer, but I'm cutting hours so I can focus on my program. Okalee never got to pursue her dream, and I feel I owe it to her to work on mine."

I nod, amazed.

"And I'm going back to school," Mrs. Mason says. "I've always wanted to write picture books and poetry for kids. I'm applying to master of fine arts programs in Vermont, Kentucky, and Minnesota. If I get in—"

"You'll get in, Mami," Wardie says. She chucks his cheek.

"If I get in," she continues, "I'll travel there twice a year and work with an adviser during each semester. The girls at the library said they'd help me set up a fundraiser so I can buy my plane tickets."

"That's really neat," I say.

"Okalee made us realize we never know how much time we have left," Mrs. Mason says. "And that we want to use that time to pursue our dreams. We aren't getting any younger, that's for sure." Mrs. Mason smooths Wardie's unruly curls, the crow's feet around her dark eyes crinkling. "Eduardo thinks we're a pair of locos."

"No, I don't." Wardie takes another tortilla from the basket. "I think it's cool what you guys are doing. Not all fifty-year-olds think like you guys do."

"Thank you for the reminder of our advancing age," Mrs. Mason teases.

"I've been doing a lot of thinking this last week about the way I do my job." Mr. Mason ladles more soup into his bowl. "Today I came across a group of people who were asking for food and money in front of a store that doesn't allow that sort of thing. Instead of writing the people a citation, I drove all four of them to Subway, got them sandwiches, and then took one of them to the hospital—he was pretty addled, probably methamphetamines—and the other three to the nearest homeless shelter. It was so easy to help, and I wish I'd been thinking that way all thirty years I've been an officer."

I wonder what he'd do if he heard my truth. I sneak a glance at Wardie, but he's looking intently at a meatball. My own spoonful of soup scalds my throat on its way down.

"We're looking forward to hearing your solo this weekend, mija," Mrs. Mason says. "Wardie tells us you have a glorious singing voice, like—what did you say, cariño?—like Alison Krauss and Adele combined?"

A blush steals up Wardie's neck. "Something like that."

I smile at the Masons, but inside I'm quaking. How many people are counting on me to sing? Dad, Wardie, the Masons, Ms. Loring, Dr. Santana, Principal Flores. Cora Henry and Helena.

But most of all, Okalee. Okalee and me.

Part of me wants to test my voice again tonight with Wardie, but the other part is terrified because what if I try to sing and nothing comes out? Maybe my voice needs a rest. Maybe if it's well rested, then on Saturday night, it can glide into the concert hall without rusty hoarseness.

After supper, I follow Wardie up the stairs to his room. Every time I come in here I'm shocked by how clean he keeps it. His bed sits against his window like mine does, but unlike mine, his is neatly made, evergreen-colored sheets tucked under the mattress. A bookshelf doubling as a nightstand is next to his bed, and in it are his alphabetically organized books, featuring titles like *Mark of the Grizzly*, *Wolves at Our Door*, *Wildflowers of Montana*, and *The Ball Is Round: A Global History of Soccer*. Topographical maps of the Spanish Creek Wilderness Area and the Greater Yellowstone ecosystem hang on his walls like pictures of family and friends. Pictures of the fox cubs he found a couple weeks ago line the wall above his enormous oak desk.

Like I always do when I come over, I sit on the edge of his desk next to a stack of old *Ranger Rick* magazines, legs hanging down. Wardie settles into the chair and turns on his computer.

"What song are you singing for the *America's Voice* audition?" He poises expectant fingers over the keyboard.

"Wardie, I don't even know if—"

"You didn't pick one yet, then? Let's pick one."

I take a deep breath. "Okay," I say. I swivel toward the computer. *Just pretend like life is normal.* That's what Wardie wants to do. So that's what I'll do too. "There's going to be a piano there, but I want to play along to a song that I sing." Might as well plan big and bold.

Wardie brightens. He navigates to YouTube. "I've been listening to 'Sweet Afton' ever since last Saturday. It makes me cry because all I can think of is Okalee."

I know this song, and so did Okalee. It's an old Robert Burns poem turned into a Scottish song. Wardie clicks a link and presses play on a video.

First, a guitar plays several chords of music that stir up all the emotions I'm holding in my heart. Then the words spill out of the computer speakers, bittersweet as the call of a mourning dove.

> *Flow gently, sweet Afton! among thy green braes,*
> *Flow gently, I'll sing thee a song in thy praise;*
> *My Mary's asleep by thy murmuring stream,*
> *Flow gently, sweet Afton, disturb not her dream.*

By the end of the song, I know it's the right one.

"It's perfect," I say to Wardie. "It even talks about blackbirds." *And rivers,* I think, and the thought drops like a stone into my belly. How can I sing a song about a river after what happened to Okalee?

But she loved the river. And the song is based on a poem.

Poetry and rivers—two of Okalee's favorite things. I have to sing it for her.

> Thou stockdove whose echo resounds thro' the glen,
> Ye wild whistling blackbirds in yon thorny den,
> Thou green-crested lapwing thy screaming forbear,
> I charge you, disturb not my slumbering Fair.

My Blackbird. She was kind, she was smart, she was sassy, and I used to resent all those things about her. But now I wish I had her back.

We go downstairs and shut ourselves in the den, where Mr. Mason's guitar rests in the corner next to a wall-to-wall bookshelf that reaches to the ceiling. Dad built that bookshelf for Mrs. Mason. He built the ladder, too. Seeing his handiwork makes me miss him fiercely.

Wardie prints the sheet music off the Internet and sets it on the stand. Mamá taught me basic guitar skills when I was little, and I think I can learn this song in time for the *America's Voice* audition on April 7. Or maybe I might create my own version of it, one even sadder and sweeter than Nickel Creek's.

Unless I go home and Mamá looks at me with that hollowed-out expression again.

I shake my head to try to dislodge that thought.

For the rest of the night and all the next day, I practice playing the song over and over again. Mrs. Mason lets Wardie stay home, and all day, he flips the pages for me without complaining, without laughing at all the mistakes my aching fingers make. It's as though we both know that I have to learn the whole song as soon as possible, because there might not be another day like this one ever again in my life.

On Friday night, I write my apology letters to Kat, Ms. Loring, and my classmates. I set them aside and crawl into bed. I'm staying in the guest bedroom next to the den, and while it's nice, I miss my own bed. I miss so much.

That night, I dream that Okalee climbs out of the river and knocks on our door, alive after this endless week. *Just kidding,* she says. River water drips from her corkscrew curls, and she holds tiny river rocks in her hands. *I'm sorry I scared you guys. I wanted to see what it would be like around here if I died, like Tom Sawyer.*

Mamá and Dad and I rush out to greet her. *Our Blackbird!* we cry. *You're here! You're safe.* Mamá flings herself at Okalee and grips her tightly. Dad's smile lights up his eyes. And when Okalee looks at me, curls framing her flushed face, I sink to my knees on the front stoop. The weathered boards push against my kneecaps. Stray pine needles scrape my shins. I open my mouth to explain, to confess, to repent, but not one sound comes out.

The only thing that breaks the terrible quiet is the call of a red-winged blackbird, harsh, mocking my silence.

I sleep until the sun streams through the window and shines in a hot patch on the quilt I'm under. The dream clings to me, and I don't try to shake it off. It was so real; Okalee was alive. No matter that she had hurt in her eyes when she looked at me. No matter that I could not speak to apologize to her.

She was alive.

I close my eyes and squeeze my fists together. I want to stay in the dream. I would endure Okalee looking at me like that for a lifetime if it meant having her back.

But then Mrs. Mason raps gently at the door and says, "Phoebe, hija, whenever you're ready, we have fresh Nutella croissants out here for breakfast."

The dream melts away, and it's like I'm watching Okalee drown all over again.

That evening, as the light in the valley begins to sink, Wardie and I squelch through the muddy grasses of the bike path next to the highway. We've decided to have some hot chocolate at the Spanish Creek Café downtown before the concert.

Grayling Crossing is tiny. The downtown is pretty much all there is: Spanish Creek Café and Wilson's Grocery tucked among the redbrick buildings to the right; a bar, an antique store, a hair salon, and a few other random places to the left. The Grayling Crossing Inn sits farther down Main Street, an imposing stone building surrounded by an army of spruce trees.

Inside the café, I glimpse a poster on the door announcing our spring concert.

COME ENJOY BEAUTIFUL MUSIC SUNG BY
THE GRAYLING CROSSING ELEMENTARY SCHOOL AT THE
25TH ANNUAL SPRING CONCERT
AT THE GRAYLING CROSSING INN
ADMISSION $5.00 PER PERSON. THE CONCERT BEGINS AT 6:00 ON MARCH 10.

Six o'clock. Only an hour and a half away. An hour and a half until I have to sing. Until I walk through the doors of the Grayling Crossing Inn and prepare to beg Okalee for forgiveness.

Wardie motions me over to the counter. The smell of cinnamon and baking bread wraps me in an embrace, and my nerves ease a tiny bit. The barista smiles at us. Will she attend the concert tonight? The concert that people are paying money to hear?

"Welcome," she says. "What can I do for you guys today?"

Wardie looks at me. "What do you want, Phoebe?"

I shake my head. I'm too nervous to decide.

He tugs his wallet out of his back pocket, and I imagine him as a gangly high school guy or a young college man, whipping out his wallet for a girlfriend. He started carrying it around in his jeans recently. I know because his back pocket isn't creased like Dad's is.

"We'll take two hot chocolates, a plain croissant, and"—he pauses, glancing at me—"a chocolate croissant. Warmed, please." He grins at me. "Today's just the day for croissants, I guess."

I know that last order is for me. The café smells remind me of Cuban coffee and, with a pang, I wonder if Mamá had passed this coffee shop when she walked through town on Thursday.

I shake the thought away and touch Wardie's hand. "I'll pay you back," I whisper as the barista starts turning knobs and steam billows behind the counter.

"No need." Wardie leaves a ten-dollar bill on the counter and wraps his arm around me. "Consider it a gift in preparation for tonight."

We walk to a table next to a window overlooking Main Street. We sit in the two chairs, and I look at this best friend of mine. He's done so much for me ever since we met, but also since March 3. I realize I've done nothing for him in return—nothing. Instead, I shoved him when he was trying to help me find Okalee.

"Wardie," I say. "Did I ever tell you I'm sorry?"

He turns his gaze on me. "What for?"

I want to look away, but I don't. "For shoving you into the dirt. The day Okalee . . ."

He looks confused, and then the memory smooths out his eyebrows. "Oh, that," he says, waving his hand. A muscle twitches in his forearm. "You probably did."

But I can't remember if I did or not. "I'm sorry I did that. You didn't deserve it."

A half smile curves his lips. "It's all right. You're not that strong anyway. The shove didn't hurt much."

I bat at his hand. "Hey!"

"I'm kidding, I'm kidding! Everyone knows you're strong."

I only wish that were true.

The barista sets down our giant mugs, the warm croissants on platters next to them. I take a sip of the sweet chocolate and close my eyes as it slides over my tongue like a bolt of silk unspooling. That makes me think about Mamá again, how she used to smell of the quilt shop where she works: like fabric and humming machines. She hasn't touched her sewing machine or her stacks of fabric all week.

This time I let my thoughts stay on my mother. I eat my croissant slowly, wondering when or if Mamá will ever go back to work. Yesterday, when Dad called the Masons' to suggest I stay one more night, he said Mamá wasn't doing well. He mentioned then that he wouldn't go back to work until he was sure she was all right.

Will she ever be all right? Will any of us?

That question spills a heavy darkness into my bones. I try to focus on the taste of the chocolate, the warmth of the croissant, the closeness of Wardie sitting next to me.

A few more people come in for coffee, the door chiming to announce their entrance, and Wardie wipes a crumb off his chin. "This is nice. No wonder people come to cafés all the time. It's relaxing."

I nod. Relaxing. Yes. I try to relax. I pretend all the threats hanging over me don't exist in this warm, quietly busy café. Maybe in a peaceful place like this, detached as it is from my life at school and my life at home, I can take a deep breath that won't hurt me.

I close my eyes and drink air into my lungs—and it does hurt, but not as much as usual—and it's in that breath of silence that I hear the voices.

15

They're women's voices, one of which I recognize instantly as Mrs. McClain's, Helena's mother.

"Helena told me she hasn't slept all week," Mrs. McClain says. She and her companion must be standing in line to order coffee.

Wardie reaches across the gap between our chairs and takes my hand. I hold his tightly.

"She doesn't blame herself, does she?" says the other woman. Her voice sounds vaguely familiar. Do I dare turn around?

I duck my chin to my chest and peek out the corner of my eye.

Kat's mother, Brandi-Michelle Waters, stands next to Mrs. McClain.

I whip back around, heart racing. I tune out all the

other sounds in the coffee shop and focus only on the conversation between Mrs. Waters and Mrs. McClain.

"I think she does," Mrs. McClain says. "She said she hopped on Bo and they sped away, and she doesn't understand why she didn't ride toward the girls instead of away from them."

Adrenaline shoots through me; my legs feel heavy and hot. Every beat of my heart is a spear piercing my body.

"Katherine's been acting strangely this week too. She said Helena told her not to tell anyone about the part where Phoebe—" Her voice lowers and I can't hear it, but my brain fills in the words: *pushed her sister in.* "But Katherine thought if she told Phoebe that particular bit of the supposed rumor, Phoebe might be unable to sing." A tired laugh. "Not her best moment."

Sweat slicks between my hand and Wardie's. His gaze is hot on my cheek, but I keep staring, unseeing, at the window.

Helena saw Okalee and me that day. That must be what Mrs. McClain means. *Helena* is the pink-hoodie girl.

And worst of all, *Helena* is the one who wrote the typed-up notes. Did she go to the library yesterday to see if I'd left my note of truth there? I didn't even think about that after my outburst during choir practice on Thursday because I was so sure Kat was the one who'd written the notes.

But she wasn't.

Helena was. And all week, she's been acting like she's still my friend.

I jump up.

"Phoebe, wait!" Wardie cries out, but the screech of my chair has already caught Mrs. McClain's attention.

She takes a step back. "Phoebe," she says softly.

"Where is she?" I don't want to make another scene, but I have to get to Helena.

Mrs. McClain brushes her reddish hair over her shoulders and straightens her spine and adjusts her purse in the crook of her elbow. "Phoebe," she says in a grown-up, no-nonsense, I've-made-you-hundreds-of-dinners voice. "I'd like you to come sit with us, if you want to talk about this."

"I've heard what I need to know," I say.

"Phoebe!" Wardie practically screeches. He jumps up and grabs my arm. "Sorry, Mrs. McClain, we're just on our way out." He drags me out the door. The cold spring air clashes against my sweaty neck.

"I bet I know where she is." I start to run.

"What are you going to do to her?" Wardie's shoes slap the sidewalk behind me, but I'm faster than he is.

A red-tailed hawk drags its *scree* through the sky. I don't answer Wardie because I don't know. All I know is that I need to see Helena.

I need to ask her if it's true.

We find Helena in the field behind the Grayling Crossing Inn. She's standing next to a lone cottonwood tree, her nose buried in Bo's mane. She's already wearing her black choir gown, and her copper hair shimmers under the long fingers of the setting sun.

"Helena." I lean over to catch my breath. Saliva spreads through my mouth, bitter as blood.

She turns, surprise alighting on her face and then slipping away when she sees it's me. She doesn't look like she has a headache anymore. She's wearing eyeliner and mascara and even a dark lipstick. She looks stunning.

And she betrayed me.

"You saw Okalee and me," I say. "You wrote me those notes. You—" I struggle to keep my voice from cracking. "You told everyone that I pushed Okalee into the river."

Helena doesn't even look shocked. It's as though she expected me to come find her. But her lower lip trembles.

"You did push her in, Phoebe." She shakes her head. "I saw you."

I take a step closer. Mud sucks at my shoes. "I did not push her. Not on purpose. I was trying to get her out of the river, but she wouldn't come. She wouldn't listen to me."

Relief unfurls on Helena's face, but my voice rises. "If you saw us, why didn't you come help?"

The relief vanishes. "Don't turn this on me. You're the one who—" She turns bright red and doesn't finish that particular sentence. "You're the one who isn't telling the truth."

"Tell me," I say. "Tell me how you saw us."

Bo nickers in Helena's ear and shuffles closer to her. She clings to his mane. "I was exercising Bo. I thought I'd take the long way to your house and see if you wanted my help to choose a song for the"—her voice cracks—"*America's Voice* audition."

She cries silently for several long seconds, and a piece of me feels sorry for her, but rage sweeps through me harder than empathy. Why didn't Helena help me? Why did she run? Why did she have to be there at all if she wasn't going to help me save my sister?

Just then, Wardie appears in my corner of my eye.

"Hey, Helena, don't cry," he says, joining us. He reaches out to touch her shoulder.

"You're supposed to be on my side!" I say to Wardie.

Wardie shakes his head. "There aren't sides. We're best friends. All of us."

"Helena's only been pretending to be my friend." I dig my toes into the mud. "She betrayed me."

"How can you say that?" Helena drops Bo's mane. "You

lied about what happened that day. What were you and Okalee even doing at the river? I bet it wasn't her idea at all to go down there. Before she walked in and you pushed her, you both looked pretty happy and cheerful. And you were wearing stuff you could swim in. *Both* of you."

The setting sun blazes in my vision, and all the fight drains out of me. My shoulders slump. I start to shiver. I think of Okalee's yellow swimsuit, of the tank top and shorts I threw in my closet on River Day and haven't been able to look at since, not even to put in the washing machine. No one in their right mind would wear something like that on a March morning in Montana for normal reasons.

"We had a tradition called River Day," I say. "And yes, I started it. Yes, it was my idea." I take a deep and painful breath. "Yes, I let my sister go into the river, and I didn't stop her. So yes." I pause. "I lied."

Helena closes her eyes. "Because you were terrified."

In that sentence I hear her truth as well as mine. I hear the reason she sped away on Bo instead of racing to help us.

Yes, I *was* terrified.

"You were too," I say.

She bites her lip. She nods.

Before either of us can say anything else, someone shouts my name. "Phoebe?" The sound is frantic. And then, "Eduardo? Where are you?"

Wardie jumps. "That's my mom." He frowns. "Something's up. We'd better go find her."

While Helena ties Bo to the cottonwood tree, Wardie and I run to the Grayling Crossing Inn parking lot.

"Maybe Ms. Loring's looking for us," I say breathlessly. "It's probably 5:30." That's when we're supposed to meet for warm-ups and final notes.

Wardie says nothing. He and I both know Mrs. Mason wouldn't sound that frantic just because Ms. Loring was looking for us.

Mrs. Mason waves us to the lawn of the Inn. Mr. Mason stands behind her, hands buried in his pockets.

"There you are," Mrs. Mason says. She rubs her forehead. "Phoebe . . . oh, I don't know how to say this."

"Say what?" I swallow hard. Concertgoers and singers mill around the parking lot and slide through the giant, castle-like doors of the Inn. Kat and her parents stand in a knot with a tall, thin man who must be the scout from Bozeman High. I don't see the 4Runner anywhere.

Where is Dad? He promised he'd come. Did Mamá convince him to stay home in a final show of disapproval about the solo?

Mr. Mason puffs a hard breath and then looks me straight in the eye. "Your mom and dad won't be able to come tonight."

"Why?"

"Your mom has been admitted to Bozeman Deaconess Hospital."

The grass drops out from under me. "What?"

"I'm sorry, Phoebe."

"Why is my mom in the hospital?" I feel dull and stupid.

Mr. Mason exchanges a glance with Mrs. Mason, and a quick, silent conversation takes place between them. "Exhaustion," he says slowly. "Related to grief."

I have become an expert liar, and I know a fellow liar when I see one. Mr. Mason swallows uncomfortably, and he's having a hard time looking me in the eye.

"You're lying," I say. "What happened?"

Mrs. Mason says, "Your dad didn't want us to tell you, querida. We'll let him tell you after—"

"Tell me. Please."

"Phoebe." Mr. Mason shakes his head firmly. "Your father wants you to sing. He asked us to record it for him to watch."

"So whatever happened is bad enough that I might not be able to sing if I knew?" My hand flails around behind me, searching for Wardie's fingers. We clasp hands. I can feel his pulse racing in his thumb.

"I . . ." Mr. Mason drags his hand over his graying hair.

"If you don't tell me, I won't sing." I feel terrible for threating Mr. Mason like this, kind Mr. Mason who helped pull Okalee from the river and who made me croissants this morning. But I have to know.

Mr. Mason sighs. His shoulders sag. "Your mother walked into the river, Phoebe."

I stare at Mr. Mason, and that's when I notice Kat Waters standing right behind him, her blue eyes wide, and I know she's heard everything. I glare at her until she backs away and disappears through the heavy wooden doors.

"Phoebe?" Mr. Mason draws my attention back to him.

"She walked into the river," I repeat, slowly. "Was she . . ." The words are too terrible to say out loud, but I know all at once that words like this must be spoken. Words like this lose some of their power if you're brave enough to push them into existence.

An odd calm fills me. "Was she trying to die?"

I brace myself for his answer.

Mr. Mason shakes his head slowly. "Your mother has really been struggling this week. Your dad thinks she was trying to, I don't know, feel Okalee's pain. Feel the river the way Okalee would've felt it right before. In the ambulance, she told him she needed to know how it happened and she couldn't think of any other way to find out." He looks sadly at me. "She said something about wanting to face her fear of the water too. That she owed it to Okalee for leaving her . . ." He clears his throat and changes the subject, embarrassed, but I hear the unspoken words anyway.

For leaving her *with me*.

My face feels hot. I can barely breathe. Mamá asked me for the truth on Thursday, and I lied to her. If I hadn't lied, if I had told the whole, terrible truth, would she still have walked into the river? Or would she have stayed on the bank, with me? Stayed away from the raging current?

Something inside me shifts. I think about how Mamá must feel, not knowing what really happened.

How terrible would it be for a mother not to know the truth about how her child died?

"Is she okay?" I gasp.

"She's stable. We can leave right now to go see her, or you can stay and sing and we'll go right after the solo."

I nod. My neck hurts. But the rest of me feels like part of the atmosphere: weightless and invisible and indistinguishable from its surroundings.

"Are you okay?" Wardie's in front of me now, concern lining his forehead.

"Estás bien, hija?" Mrs. Mason touches my shoulder, then looks at her husband. "I knew we shouldn't have told her. Lars isn't going to be happy."

Mr. Mason looks at the ground.

"Thank you. For telling me." I square my shoulders, shake away the image of Mamá wading into the Grayling River. Shake away all the other truths that cling to that image.

I must move forward. I must sing for Okalee. Now more than ever before, I must get her forgiveness.

"We'd better go," I say to Wardie. "We don't want Ms. Loring to worry."

I change into my choir dress, drink some water, and move woodenly through the warm-up exercises. Kat and Wardie and Helena all keep looking at me, all for different reasons I am sure, but I keep my focus on Ms. Loring's flushed face, her swinging baton.

At five minutes to six, we line up in the rehearsal room behind the concert hall stage. The lights in there are dim. A low, expectant murmur echoes from inside. Ms. Loring hands us each a candle.

Dr. Santana walks up to me, smiling. "Phoebe, how are you feeling today?"

She doesn't know about Mamá. "Ready to sing," I say with an easy smile.

I tell myself—

Don't think about Mamá.

Just think about Okalee.

Just sing.

She looks at me closely, seems to decide something, and pats my shoulder. "Glad to hear it."

"All right," Ms. Loring says to the group. "It's almost

time." She scampers by, lighting all the candles with her own long candlestick. Then she adjusts Wardie's and Cora's microphones that are clipped to their chests. When she fiddles with mine, her fingers nervous against my dress collar, she whispers, "You can do this, Phoebe. I believe in you!"

So many people believe in me. Do I believe in myself?

Does Okalee believe in me?

Ms. Loring pauses in front of the whole upper-grade choir. "Okay, everyone, I'm headed to the piano. Is everyone ready?"

"Yes, Ms. Loring," we say in unison.

She looks directly at me and gives me a thumbs-up. I ignore the voices of doubt and fear screaming in my brain and raise my thumb in return.

She grins. "You're all going to be great!"

Then she vanishes into the black mouth beyond the rehearsal room door.

Mr. Ripwinkle stands in the doorway. A hush falls over the crowd inside the auditorium, and then Mr. Ripwinkle motions us forward. I lead the way.

Swish, swish. The sound of dresses moving. *Clack, clack.* The sound of shoes stepping.

I step across the threshold. Hundreds of eyes stare up at me. My candle flickers, illuminating noses and mouths and smiling teeth. Mr. Mason crouches in front of the stage, video camera in hand.

Cora's clear voice pours into the stillness. I watch my candle shiver and sway, and pain burns through me. It's not just my pain, I realize. It's Mamá's pain, Mamá's anguish.

Wardie's deeper voice follows Cora's. I stare at the burning wick. The minute of silence is both an eternity and an instant.

Ms. Loring plays my opening notes.

Then there is silence.

I am supposed to break this silence. Here is where I sing to my sister. Here is where my voice tells her how sorry I am for everything I've done to her in the last week. Here is the moment I've been fighting for ever since I lost her in that river, ever since the big and terrible lie came oozing out of my mouth.

I scan the waiting faces for Mamá and Dad and then remember—*whoosh!* my breath leaves my chest—that they aren't here.

That's all right, I tell myself. It's only Okalee that matters.

Is it?

Honey is sliding down my throat, honey and sweet almond oil. My voice is tucked into my diaphragm. It's waiting for me to give it the cue to rise up and pour out of me.

I open my mouth, and my voice is just like the other day, scratchy and rusty and dying.

As I went down in the river to pray,
Studying about that good old way
And who shall wear the starry crown
Good Lord, show me the way.

I stop, breath quick and heavy.

This is really happening. I am really failing at singing my apology to my sister—again.

A bad kind of quiet steals into the auditorium, the kind of quiet that says the crowd is embarrassed for me.

I have to try again. I steady myself, but something shifts in the rows of students around me. I hear Wardie whisper, "Hey!"

Then someone pokes my back, and I turn. Kat stands behind me. She looks me full in the face.

I'm confused. She's supposed to be in her place toward the back of the line.

"Kat!" Wardie exclaims. "Go back to your spot." His whisper is urgent.

Kat says nothing. She inches closer, her shoes squeaking on the shiny floors.

The spotlight on me starts to bloom into brightness, showing me Ms. Loring's panicked face at the piano. She is still playing, but I know she is stalling. I'm supposed to have sung the second verse by now.

Kat leans close to my ear, so close that her breath

tickles my skin. In a teeny tiny voice she whispers, "You can't sing because you let your sister drown and then lied about it. Your sister would hate you."

My terrible creaky singing voice slides down my throat and drops into the pit of my belly.

I whip around. My elbow bends. My fingers coil into a fist.

The truth of Kat's words builds in my elbow, my arm, builds until it has nowhere left to go but out.

I draw my fist back and slam it into Kat's face. My knuckle stings as her nose crumples beneath it.

There's a loud, horrified gasp, and it's coming from everyone in the whole audience. The piano makes a horrible sound as Ms. Loring stops playing. Blood trickles from Kat's nostrils and onto her bright-pink lipstick.

Your sister would hate you.

I didn't mean to fail Okalee. I didn't mean to let her die. I didn't mean to send Mamá into the river looking for answers. I didn't mean to break Dad's heart.

I hate me too, Okalee.

I *hate* me.

Before this moment I never knew I could despise myself like *this*. I want to crawl out of my body, run screaming from the ugliness inside.

I push through the crowd, away from Wardie, Mr. Mason, and Dr. Santana, who're rushing toward Kat and me. I don't look at anyone or anything. I focus on the space in front of me as I shove past Mr. Ripwinkle and into the foyer. I burst into the cold spring evening.

The sun has descended behind Lone Peak, and the world is gray giving way to black.

I run.

16

I run faster than I ever have in my life.

My legs carry me down Main Street, left on Cottonwood Road, past Grayling Crossing Elementary School, and into the field that leads to my house.

Run, Phoebe, run. Run, run, Phoebe.

The trees whisper my name.

I run away from Kat and her words of truth and her bloody nose, away from everyone in the crowd at the Inn. Away from the Grayling River and the ghost of Mamá walking in to find out how Okalee died.

But more than anything, I run away from Okalee broken, Okalee mad, Okalee hating me.

Blackbird, Blackbird, what have I done?

My lungs burn, and something metallic pools on my tongue. The trail rises before me, the foothills black against the sky. I slow to a jog.

If I thought running would ease the hollowed-out, screaming feeling of self-hatred, I was wrong. It yanks at my shoulders, trying to twist me back toward the Inn. Toward the people who know the real and horrible me.

I start running again.

The moon against the clouds gives me the palest light.

THUMP-thump-THUMP-thump-THUMP-thump.

O sister, keep on running.

O sinner, do not stop.

The wind can howl through the spruces all it wants.

I will not stop.

I come to a low, spruce-covered hill and stagger to my knees. *Just a short break.* This hate is crushing me; it wants to mash me into the dirt. It wants to crunch my face against fallen pine needles.

Then a snuffling sound comes from the hill above, and I look straight into the gold eyes of a wolf.

I am rooted like a spruce tree. This wolf is maybe a Dad-length away from me.

She blinks. She stands tall and strong. Her gray coat shimmers in the moonlight. She shuffles her paws and sits like a dog would.

Go ahead, I think. *Attack me. I deserve it.*

But the wolf tilts her nose to the sky, neck long and

white and graceful. A mournful howl rises from her throat, and in that wild sound I hear the words *You'll find her at the river*.

Okalee wants me to find her.

Before the howl ends, I take off, splitting away from the trail and to the right, where I know the Grayling is laughing and rushing on its way toward my house and the Oxtail Bridge and Yellowstone.

I tear through the aspens and the spruces and the tangling grasses, and the river laughs louder and louder until the laugh turns into a roar.

And suddenly I am there. I almost fall in because there's no smooth bank of grass and stones here like there is at home. There's just spruce trees, a hunk of earth, and then the current. I kneel, my skirt sinking into the wet dirt.

"Okalee?" I stare across the river. All I see is black water, black trees, black sky. "Okalee? It's Phoebe. I'm here." My eyes fall to the current, trying to see through it. The river skips over boulders and swirls around rocks, and then it talks to me.

You let her die. You pushed her into me, and you drowned her in my waters.

"I didn't mean to."

You were jealous of her. You were selfish.

"I know." My fingernails pierce the dirt. The branches above me slap and hiss and shiver. "You're right."

And that's not the worst of it. You shamed her memory too. You lied about how she died, and your mother knows it, and your mother can't stand not to know the truth.

"I know," I say. That hollowed-out, screaming feeling gets so bad that I want a stiff wind to shove me into the river and mash me down to the bottom.

No. You do not want that. That is not the answer.

Everything inside of me goes still. I have been lying so much lately that I almost don't recognize it as the truth, but the river is right.

The only way to heal from this self-hatred I feel is to leave behind the lies and speak the truth.

A light wind stirs the forest. *Shh, shh,* it says, and then I hear it—an urgent, frantic voice. "Phoebe? Phoebe!"

I listen hard. "Wardie?"

"Phoebe! Where are you?"

"I'm over here." I raise my voice. "I'm here by the river."

I stand and rest my head against the trunk of a cottonwood tree next to the riverbank. The bumpy bark rubs against my skull. With my face turned into the wind, I take a huge breath and shout, "I'm here!"

"Where?"

He crashes through the spruces, a bobbing dot of light. The trees murmur and sway as he emerges.

"What are you doing?" He grabs my shoulders and yanks me toward the spruces. "Get away from the river!" Wardie's crying. I've never seen him cry like this before.

"I'm away," I say, reaching out to him. "It's okay, Wardie."

The wind surges between us. I touch his snotty, damp shirtsleeve. "I can't find Okalee. She won't talk to me. I can't even hear her voice in my head. In my dreams she's angry with me, Wardie."

Wardie takes big, deep breaths. The moonlight glints off the salt tracks lining his cheeks.

"I don't know what to do," I say.

The wind pauses.

Then a red-winged blackbird sings *o-ka-lee, o-ka-lee, o-ka-lee*, and for the first time since Okalee drowned, the blackbird is not mocking me, not blaming me for what happened to Okalee. This time, I hear in that warbling trill what I need to do to find her again. I want to drop to the ground with the relief of it, but instead I look at the tattered and muddy hem of my choir dress.

Wardie wipes his eyes. "We should get—"

"I lied to you." My voice barely rises above the wind.

Wardie goes still. "What?"

The river glides past us, just beyond the branches. The

river that let us celebrate spring and sisterhood and me being better than Okalee at something big.

"You know how I told you that when she surfaced that one time, before she . . ." I try to slow my racing breath. "Before I never saw her again—remember how I said her eyes were closed?"

"Yeah?" Wardie leans toward me, focused and waiting. The wind rattles the branches. I take a deep breath of the windy, rivery, muddy air.

Here is the place where I've lied to Wardie and Dr. Santana and, most importantly, to myself. Here is the truth my brain keeps trying to remind me about. Here is the truth I have pushed deep into my body.

"They weren't." I squeeze my eyes shut. I remember what I really saw: Okalee with her eyes wide open, begging me to save her. "I was only maybe four feet away, but the current was so strong." Tears push against my eyes, hot and prickling. "She looked straight at me, and her eyes said 'Please. Save me, please.'

"I froze. I screamed for her. It was only for a split second, but I could have lunged and maybe grabbed her before it was too late, but I couldn't believe what was happening. That look in her eyes . . ." I shudder at the memory.

"Then I did lunge, but by then the river had already started yanking her under again. I swam so hard. I screamed because it hurt my arms and legs and stomach so much to fight the river, to swim toward my sister."

Pain pushes against my throat. *Say it. Say what really happened.*

"I grabbed her wrist." Bitter tears stream over my open lips and prick my tongue. Her cold, skinny, beautiful wrist. "My fingers clamped around it. She had such relief in her eyes, and I thought I had her. I thought I could pull her out of the current and swim her safe to shore."

I pause, and the feeling of horror that swept over me then fills me again now. "But then the current tore her out of my grasp. It just tore her away from me. I screamed her name and I was crying and she gave me one last look before she disappeared, and that's when I knew. I knew that she knew what was happening to her."

I collapse to my knees and hug myself tight. Wardie stands next to me, his hand on my shoulder. I cry for a long time, tears salty in my mouth. When all the tears are spent, I whisper, "How can I live with myself?"

"I'm so sorry."

"I can't forget her eyes looking at me like that, so hopeless, knowing she was drowning, knowing I couldn't save her."

"But Phoebe," Wardie says, "she wasn't blaming you."

The wind stops blowing, and the trees stop whispering. Everything is still.

He kneels down next to me, and his face is warm and glowing and earnest. "You tried to save her. It was the river's fault she died. Not yours. Not hers." Wardie's dark curls flutter in the breeze. "It was an accident. The worst accident."

One that could have been avoided, I think. But that's not direct enough.

One that I could have prevented.

But I didn't.

And Okalee, she's passed away.

My Blackbird, she's dead.

My lip trembles again, and I can't stop the tugging, aching sadness from taking over my body. "She's really gone," I say, gasping, crying again. "She's not here anymore."

Wardie shakes his head. "But she loved you, Phoebe. And I know you loved her."

The wolf's faraway howl soars steadily into the night.

"I'll always love her."

17

An hour later, I walk toward Mamá's hospital room at Bozeman Deaconess. Wardie, Helena, and Mrs. Mason wait in the lobby, but Officer Mason and Dr. Santana walk on either side of me. Officer Mason is wearing his police uniform because his night shift starts as soon as he's done here with me. Dr. Santana lays her hand on my shoulder, and the warmth of her fingers steadies my racing heart.

The ride here was silent except for when I asked Officer Mason to join me in the hospital room, as I had something to say that he'd need to hear. Dr. Santana asked me if I wanted her to come too. I think she knows what I am about to do.

And now here I am.

"Room 103," Officer Mason says. He smiles sadly and nods at Mamá's closed door.

I take a deep breath, which still hurts my lungs and my heart and every splinter of bone inside me, but I think that's something I'm going to have to learn to live with.

I knock, my knuckles soft against the wood. Dad opens the door almost immediately, and when he sees me, his face breaks into a smile.

"Phoebe," he says. "How did your solo go?"

I shake my head. Dad looks at Officer Mason, but I don't have time to interpret their glances because right then I see Mamá.

She's connected to all sorts of cords and wires. A monitor beeps with every beat of her heart. A feeding tube snakes into her mouth, and my own throat chokes as though I am the one with a tube jammed into my body.

Mamá watches me, her dark eyes filled with pain. What hurts her more—the machines and the tube, or seeing me, the one who put her in that bed?

Dad's hand lands on my shoulder. "Your mom has very low blood sugar levels, but she couldn't eat. That's why . . ." He gestures to the tube. "And she's badly dehydrated." A big bag drips clear liquid into the veins of Mamá's hand.

"I have something to tell you." I make myself look into my mother's eyes. "All of you."

Officer Mason comes around the side of the bed. Dr. Santana squeezes my hand.

Dad stays where he is. "Whenever you're ready, my girl, we'll be listening."

And so I start at the very beginning, with the story of how I came up with River Day as a way to show Okalee I could do something better than she could. How it turned into that, but also into a tradition to celebrate spring and sisterhood. How she said she wanted to go alone this time and I said no, and then, on the morning of our very last River Day together, she distracted me and charged into the river when I wasn't looking.

How I froze. How I tried to grab her elbow but she yanked her arm away and fell instead, thinking I'd shoved her. How I got so mad I let her get all the way to the boulder.

How I realized she was in danger and ran into the river to help her.

How I was too late to keep her from going under the first time.

How I swam close enough to see her pleading, open eyes when she surfaced; how I froze with horror; how I reached out and had her—*I had a hold of her*—but the river ripped us apart.

How she knew she was drowning.

Though I'm talking to all four of them, I keep my gaze on Mamá. She is the one who needs this truth the most.

Tears spill silently onto the oxygen tubes, the feeding tube, the pale, dry skin stretched over her collarbone.

"I'm so sorry," I say when I'm done. "It's my fault she died, and it's my fault you're here, Mamá."

She turns her cheek to the side so she's not looking at me anymore.

I know I deserve this. I know I do. But a hollow ache, powerful and intense, sweeps through me, and it leaves me weak and light-headed. I feel like I'm going to fall over. For a moment, no one speaks.

Then Officer Mason wipes the corners of his eyes. Dad uses a washcloth to clean Mamá's face. Dr. Santana whispers, "You did it, Phoebe," in my ear, but I don't feel relief, and I don't feel pride.

Dad turns to me. I look for anger, for blame, for the hatred I have dreaded seeing in his kind blue eyes.

But it's not there.

"It's not your fault, sweetheart," Dad says. "None of this is."

I don't deserve this grace. "But it is, Dad. I made up the tradition. It was my idea to cross the river even though it was so high. I should have put a stop to it before we ever walked down that morning."

Dad kneels in front of me so I can see his whole face. He cups my cheeks in his warm, big palms, and the touch, the smell of wood shavings and aftershave, and the deep love in his voice makes me cry.

"You couldn't have known something like that would happen. But she made the choice to go in, and the river was too strong for the two of you. You kids, you think you're invincible. That's just part of being young." His eyes widen. "Believe me, Phoebe. Please."

"Okay," I whisper. "I believe you." I'll say it over and over in my mind, for the rest of my life, until I actually do. I smile, but it's a shaky one.

Dad stands up, and I turn to Officer Mason. I don't want to look at Mamá again, don't want to see what's written on her face. "I lied to you." I straighten my shoulders and prepare to face justice. "That's a crime. 'Montana Code Annotated 45-7-205. False reports to law enforcement authorities.'"

Officer Mason raises his eyebrows. "Yes," he says slowly. "You did lie."

"Are you going to arrest me now?" I ask. Dad's arm twines around me, and I lean into his warm chest.

"Well," Officer Mason says, "everyone in this room can see how sorry you are, Phoebe. You lied because you were scared. And now you've told the truth."

"But I need to pay," I say. "I need to pay for what I've done."

"Oh, sweet girl." Officer Mason grips my shoulder and looks right into my eyes. "You've already paid enough."

I can't speak.

"More than enough," Dad agrees.

Mamá is still turned away from me.

I need her to see me. I need to hear something from her. I step forward and kneel on the harsh white linoleum.

Dad starts murmuring something to Officer Mason and Dr. Santana, and I'm grateful for the privacy.

"Mamá?" I whisper.

Mamá slides her gaze toward me.

"Lo siento," I croak. "Lo siento tanto." I take hold of her hand, bony like Okalee's, and clutch it tight. "Perdóname si puedes."

Please forgive me, Mamá. I would understand if she didn't. But I want my mother back. I want us to tie aprons around our waists and bake lemon bars in memory of Okalee. I want us to stand hip to hip and hem to hem in the kitchen, sipping thick, bittersweet Cuban coffee and talking about how much we miss Okalee's golden head bent over her schoolwork.

But Mamá doesn't squeeze my hand back. She looks at me, her head shaking slightly, and I feel cold all over.

So this is how my life will be now.

I turn away and run into Dad's arms as though I'm a five-year-old kid.

He holds me close. "Give her time, love. Give her time."

I thought my tears had run dry, but in Dad's arms, I cry and cry and cry.

18

I stay with the Masons for two weeks. Dad comes to see me every day after he gets home from work and the hospital, but every time he asks if I want to see Mamá, I say no. He tells me about her improvements anyway: after a few days, the feeding tube is removed, and though Mamá eats, she hardly talks. She's getting better at staying hydrated. She sees a psychiatrist every day who is helping Mamá figure out what medications are best for stabilizing her mind.

I tuck all this information away in a box in my heart with Mamá's name carved on the lid, and then I try not to think about it.

I earn a week's suspension from school for punching Kat. She ended up grabbing some tissues and an ice pack for her nose and insisted on singing for the scout after all. He must have liked what he heard because he agreed to save her a spot in the Bozeman High School choir, just like she always wanted.

I won't ever punch someone like that again, and I even told Kat I was sorry, but I have this feeling Okalee approves of what I did. I have a feeling she knows Kat deserved it.

Officer Mason refused to report me to the authorities, but he helped me contact the *Bozeman Daily News* to correct the news story, as though they'd gotten it wrong from the start. And he gave me the idea of doing something in Okalee's honor.

Okalee wanted to be a pediatric nurse when she grew up. So every Tuesday afternoon, I go to the children's cancer ward at the hospital and read picture books to the kids who are suffering and living out their childhoods between hospital walls. Sometimes Wardie comes with me, and we bring Bunny for the kids to pet and kiss and whisper their painful secrets to.

When the kids ask me if I have any siblings, I take a deep and aching breath and tell them about my sister, Okalee.

Other afternoons, I walk in the forest with Wardie or gallop on horses at Helena's ranch or ride my bike through the firming fields and blooming flowers, plucking some to take to Okalee's grave. There, I talk to her as though she's still with me. I tell her how Ms. Loring gives me free voice lessons every Wednesday, helping me steady my voice and widen the range it can soar or plunge. I tell her how Helena and I talked about everything that happened, how we both apologized, and how we are now slowly getting back to normal, whatever that means.

I tell her how much I miss her. And sometimes I swear I can hear the tiny whisper of her voice exclaiming *Really?* or *That sounds fun* or even, once, *I miss you too, sis.*

Most evenings, I watch old episodes of *America's Voice* on Wardie's computer, taking notes on what the judges say, jotting down ideas for my own performance. I practice "Sweet Afton" on Wardie's guitar, spilling my voice into the lamp-lit den. It's not the singing voice it was before Okalee died, but it's getting there.

Slowly.

Then, it's April 7. A Saturday. The day of the *America's Voice* audition. There are more people packed into the Gallatin Valley Mall than I expected, and doubts start to crowd my head. It's only been a month since Okalee died.

"There's no way I can win this," I say to Wardie and Helena. "My voice isn't really that great anymore."

"Believe me, it is," Helena says. "You just can't hear how good it is. I think it's better than before."

"All you have to do is sing." Wardie gives me a

thumbs-up, then leans in and whispers, "Sing like Okalee's watching you."

Together the three of us walk to the booth to pick up my name tag. The Masons are somewhere in the crowd, and Dad's driving over as soon as he checks on Mamá like he always does now after work. She's been out of the hospital and back at home for a week, but aside from the one tiny hug she gave me the day she came home, she hasn't really left her room or talked to me. I know she needs her space.

"Phoebe Paz Petersen," I say to a lady with bright-red lipstick. She searches through a bundle of name tags in a file box and tugs out mine.

"Here you go," she says. "You're contestant number twenty-two. You'll wait backstage with all the other contestants, and we'll let you know when to go out, all right, sweet pea?"

"Ma'am?" I say hesitantly. She blinks up at me. "How many contestants are there?"

"Fifty," she chirps.

I expect the time backstage to drag, but it doesn't. I keep my mind on Okalee and what she would say if she were sitting with me right now.

You got this, Phoebe. Think about the poem: "When you feel afraid, remember; Where one tree falls, more can grow."

You're a new tree now, sis. Rise up, and be strong.

Before I feel completely ready, the backstage manager says, "Contestant number twenty-two, you're on next." He ushers me up to the backside of the curtain. I clutch the guitar. A few of the other contestants, mostly young people like me, whisper, "Good luck."

"The microphone should be ready to go," the man tells me. "The judges are right down in front of everyone. They'll be asking you questions after your performance just like they do on *America's Voice*. Are you ready?"

I nod. The old excitement that used to race through me at the beginning of a challenge courses through me now, making my hands sweaty, my legs jittery.

Contestant number twenty-one says something to the judges, and they laugh. What feels like an instant later, the manager says, "Now!"

"I'm doing this for you, Blackbird," I whisper.

I walk onto the stage. Helena did my makeup: a dash of eyeliner, spruce-green eye shadow, and ruby-red lipstick. Mrs. Mason parted my hair to one side and slipped a head-band lined with wire flowers into it.

I stand in front of the microphone, clutching the neck of the guitar. But before I begin, I scan the crowd for the faces I love, and there they are: Dr. Santana, Cora and Gracie Henry, and Ms. Loring, who spent hours helping me prepare for this moment. Wardie, Helena, Mr. and Mrs. Mason.

Dad gives me a tiny wave. He looks oddly happy. He's beaming, actually, and in the next second I see why.

Mamá stands beside him, wearing all black. Her hair falls on her shoulders in bouncy curls. Her cheeks look fuller than they did two weeks ago, and a hint of pink runs through them.

She meets my gaze, and her eyes go soft. She gives me a tiny smile, and in it I read the words *Te quiero mucho, Phoebe. I don't know what comes next, but I love you.*

The box in my heart with her name on it bursts open, and I blink and blink to keep the tears away.

Keep it together. Play for your sister.

So, with a nod to that big family of mine in the crowd, I play and I sing.

My voice still has some rasp left to it, and a mournful tone weaves through it, a tone that wasn't there before. But it's my voice, and I know Okalee would say it's stunning.

But the best part, for me, is the way I lose myself in the music. I feel like I'm bobbing above the pain of the last month. I feel alive.

> *Flow gently, sweet Afton, among thy green braes,*
> *Flow gently, sweet river, the theme of my lays;*
> *My Mary's asleep by thy murmuring stream,*
> *Flow gently, sweet Afton, disturb not her dream.*

I sing, and something strikes me as my voice surges into the audience. By doing this thing that I love, that my sister loved to listen to, I am pouring all my trapped love into the space my sister left behind.

In song, the love has somewhere to go.

"Disturb not her dream," I sing again, holding and holding the final note.

My voice sounds strong and clear and uniquely mine. But there's a roughness to it, a hollowness.

And in that moment, I know that this Okalee-sized hole left behind by my lost Blackbird will always be with me. It will always show through in my voice, in the me after Okalee.

But I also know that she's not really gone. She'll always be with me. The flash of her curls will be in the golden rays of a setting sun. Her loud laugh will echo in the trill of a red-winged blackbird. I will brush the petal of a daisy and feel like it's her skin I'm touching.

This is who I am now.

All along I was begging for Okalee to forgive me, when what I really needed was to learn to forgive myself. I know it will take time to heal, but I also know that I'll be okay.

Okalee was light. And I am at peace.

ACKNOWLEDGMENTS

This idea first came to me when I was twelve years old, so you can imagine how many wonderful people have influenced and strengthened this story along the way. Whether directly or indirectly, each of you has influenced my life and my book in meaningful ways.

Thank you, thank you, thank you.

Danielle Chiotti, the best agent in the world: thank you for believing in me and for the many notes and suggestions that dramatically improved this book. (Like, seriously. It would never have seen the light of day without you, and I wouldn't have wanted it to.) In you, I found an editor, an advocate, and a cheerleader at the same time. What a dream! I'm so grateful, and I've learned so much from you.

Lisa Mangum, my excellent, insightful editor: your suggestions and edits were spot on. Every single one. I'm still in awe at how you made the book's ending lines just perfect. Thank you so much for choosing this story and for taking such good care of Phoebe, Okalee, and me.

Chris Schoebinger, publishing director extraordinaire: thank you so much for your enthusiasm and support in shepherding this book through the publication process. Your passion for this story has amazed and delighted me since day one.

To the team at Shadow Mountain—Heidi Taylor Gordon, Rachael Ward, Richard Erickson, Troy Butcher, Callie Hansen, Ilise Levine, and Haley Huffaker—thank you so much for the hard work you put into making this a real, live book and getting it out into the world. I'm forever grateful. And thank you *so much* to Richard Erickson and Sheryl Dickert Smith for creating the most gorgeous cover. I still can't stop staring at it. It's just beautiful, and it captures the story so well.

Thank you also to Elise McMullen-Ciotti for the sensitivity read and for your notes about the setting. They were spot on.

To Georgeline Morsette: you are a star. Thank you so much for letting Cora and Gracie be Chippewa Cree and for reading the parts of the manuscript with these girls in it. Any inaccuracies in representation are my own. And thank you from the bottom of my heart for writing a poem for this book and becoming a character in it. Your creativity and activism are a light to this world.

Christiane Joy Allison, thank you for reading the entire manuscript with an eye toward grief and trauma. You never cease to amaze me. You're a talented author, tireless advocate, and wonderful critique group partner. Thank you also to Kathi Fiedler and Wendy Brooker for your friendship. You're both wonderful writers, and I treasure our pre-pandemic critique group days. To the entire Alaska SCBWI community: thank you. You're a talented bunch.

Sari Fordham, Dr. Winona Howe, and Dr. Sam McBride, my greatest writing teachers at La Sierra University: the skills you taught me about how to put my ideas into rough drafts and revise, revise, revise have been invaluable. Thank you also to Dr. Andrew Howe, Dr. Melissa Brotton, and Dr. Marilyn Loveless for teaching me so much about story, writing, and seeing something through to the end.

Susan Fletcher, Kekla Magoon, Tim Wynne-Jones, and An Na, my advisors at Vermont College of Fine Arts: each of you taught me to refine and strengthen my storytelling in countless ways. Thank you for the honest critiques and genuine support of my work.

Ashley Walker, Dianne Matich, and Stephen Baker, VCFA classmates and some of the earliest readers of this novel: thank you for your friendship and your smart in-sights into this story.

To every workshop leader, peer, and friend at VCFA's Writing for Children and Young Adults program (shout-out to the Themepunks and Harried Plotters!): thank you for your support and friendship. You helped make my years at VCFA some of the best in my life.

Also, shout-out to Jacqui Lipton, Ann Malaspina, Tina Sun Walton, Michele Andersen-Heroux, Kristy Everington, Dianne Matich, Ashley Walker, and every-one else in the Betsy's Bed and Breakfast crew—our pan-cake breakfasts, lively discussions, and trips to The Skinny Pancake are forever etched in my heart. (We really need to re-create those times one of these days!) Thank you to Kathryn Benson for doing all the writerly things with me when I lived in Tulsa. If any of you ever visit Alaska, give me a call!

My students at TAA, especially Kristen Cross, Haille Hughes, Sommer Mather, Tayler Jones, Sadi Ellis, Abdiel Pérez, and Caleb Whittington: I couldn't have asked for a better crew of then-teenagers to teach for the first time ever. Thank you for cheering me on as a writer, a teacher, and a person. Each one of you has a bright future ahead, and I'm so glad to know you.

Lora Holmes, fellow writer and longtime friend: thank you for always making it clear that it was *cool* to read and create stories. I miss you, I love you, and I need to visit Montana soon so we can see each other again!

Katy Foster, my kindred spirit friend that I wish I'd met years sooner: our adventures in Europe are among my favorite memories. I have never laughed more in my life than I did on that trip. Thank you for your friendship and for listening to me blather on about my book ideas. You will be the most knowledgeable, empathetic doctor any patient ever visited.

To all my Montana, California, Oklahoma, and Alaska friends: thank you all for being in my life and giving me an idea of what a family-like community can mean.

And a special shout-out to the Mat-Su Moms for Social Justice: I'm so grateful for each of you and for all the work you do to make our community a better, safer place for everyone. You each inspire me, and I feel lucky to count you among my friends.

My parents-in-law, Carol Najera and Josue Najera: thank you for your constant belief, support, and acceptance of me during the many stages of personhood I've gone through since we met. I love you both so much. Ellie Najera and Lance Najera, thank you for the good times when we were kids in Montana, and for all the memories and laughter we've shared since. Louann Cofrancesco and Minnette Gregg and Beth Najera—thank you for being wonderful aunts to my kid. I always love spending time with you.

To Grandpa Najera and Elena (Nana) Najera: Muchas gracias por asegurarse de que todos sienten su amor. Nana, tus tortillas son las mejores del mundo entero. Juanita Velarde, thank you for opening your home to me when I was a young college student and for being an awesome great-grandma to Abel.

To my abuelita, Dulce Ojeda Santos, and my papi-abuelo, Pedro F. Ojeda: gracias por su amor y sus historias de la vida en Cuba, Jamaica, Puerto Rico, y más. Los quiero muchísimo.

Evelyn Strawn and Donald Strawn—aka Mormor and Poppy—thank you for the cousin trips, the lefse Thanksgivings and Christmases, the many good conversations, and for stepping in as parents during my dad's cancer year. I love you both! Thank you to all my aunts, uncles, and cousins on my Strawn side for contributing to an adventure-filled childhood.

And thank you to my awesome Cuban primas for a memorable visit to Florida ten (!) years ago. I'm so glad social media has allowed us to stay in touch!

Noel Ojeda and Liz Ojeda, thank you for your support and love throughout the years.

Jeanne Troquier and Weixuan Zhang: you're both my sisters forever. I miss you both and can't wait to get together again soon. And Sammy Miklos, thank you for being a big brother for a year to Little A and for saying you'd read this book if it ever got published.

Anita Strawn de Ojeda, my mamá, a writer in her own right, and also my high school English teacher, for giving me plenty of opportunities to read, to write, and even to sell my earliest books to you for a quarter. Writing retreats with you are the absolute best; let's do them together forever. Te quiero mucho!

Pedro Ojeda, my papá: thank you for teaching me Spanish and for finding ways to make sure I was in touch with my Cuban heritage even when we lived in Montana. We *will* go to Cuba together someday soon. Te quiero mucho!

Sarah Mahl, my sister and the singer of the family: growing up with you was full of adventure, amazing made-up games, and unforgettable heart-to-hearts. Thank you for keeping my earliest secrets and for being my first best friend. I love you! And Henrique Mahl, thank you for being an awesome brother-in-law. Hanging out with the two of you is always a fun (and funny!) time.

Louis Melchor, thank you for supporting me every step of the way and for letting me escape to my little office (and to hotels) to work on this book. I can't thank you enough. I love you.

Abel Forest Melchor, my beautiful son. You transformed

my life in every good way. In so many ways you're the reason this book made it this far. Your creativity, humor, adventurousness, and love are a shining light in my world. I love you forever, sunshine.

To every writer and author whose work I've ever read and loved: there are hundreds of you, and each one influenced my life in indelible ways. Thank you for doing what you do.

And last but far from least, to my readers. Thank you for taking a chance on baby-author me and for stepping into Phoebe and Okalee's world for a time. I am forever grateful.

DISCUSSION QUESTIONS

1. In Chapter 1, Phoebe expresses her desire to win the solo for the school's spring concert. She wants to finally get a good grade on something, but her needs seem to go deeper than that. What are some reasons you think Phoebe wants the solo so badly?

2. Kat clearly wants the solo, too. She doesn't treat her teachers or classmates very well in her quest to sing the solo. Why might this opportunity be so important to her? What emotions and experiences do you think are behind Kat's anger?

3. What do you think about Phoebe and Okalee's sister tradition, River Day? Do you have any traditions that you do with your family? What are they like? What makes them special?

4. On page 68, there's a poem by Chippewa Cree poet Georgeline Morsette. Read the poem aloud alone or

together with your reading group. What do you feel when you read it? What are your favorite lines, and why?

5. After what happens with Okalee, Phoebe loses her singing voice. What are your top three reasons for why her voice was lost? How do you think Phoebe could get it back?

6. On page 153, Phoebe makes a big decision about telling the truth to Wardie. Have you ever had to tell a difficult truth to a friend? How did it make you feel? What was the result?

7. Think about the setting for the story. What three places in the fictional world of Grayling Crossing, Montana, do you think are the most important to the story? Why?

8. What five words would you use to describe *Missing Okalee*? What reasons can you give for choosing the words you did?